INKSPELL'S
Enchanted Holidays
A collection of short stories

Liz Ashlee  A. D. Brazeau  Laurel Houck

Libby Kay  Melissa Koslin  Mark Love

Tammy Mannersly  Jennifer Raines  Christina Rhoads

Inkspell's Enchanted Holidays
Copyright © 2025 Inkspell Publishing- Liz Ashlee, A. D. Brazeau, Laurel Houck, Libby Kay, Melissa Koslin, Mark Love, Tammy Mannersly, Jennifer Raines, and Christina Rhoads.

All rights reserved.

ISBN: (ebook) 978-1-964636-57-3
(print) 978-1-964636-58-0

Inkspell Publishing
207 Moonglow Circle #101
Murrells Inlet, SC 29576

Edited By Melissa Keir
Cover art By Emily's World By Design

TABLE OF CONTENTS

DEDICATION

For the fans…

Dashing Through

A Love in Motion Series Short

By Liz Ashlee

DASHING THROUGH-
EPILOGUE

"Are your eyes closed?"

I wince, in the middle of setting a plate on our dining room table, totally unprepared for whatever it is my husband has up his sleeve. I've been married to J.D. Pritchard for over a year, but he still manages to surprise me. I never know what to expect when he flashes his trademark smirk and slinks away like a cartoon villain. "Yes?"

"If you're lying, I'll bend you over that table and spank you until there's a handprint on your ass." A pause, then, "I've never thought about tattooing my hand on your ass. Let's pin that for later."

I press my lips together to keep from smiling. Pritch is – and will always be – ridiculous. I've gotten better at identifying if the words that come out of his mouth are the truth or shock value. Tattooing his hand on my butt is the latter—or at least I hope so. He would, however, definitely follow through with the spanking. Sex with Pritch is...well, not vanilla *at all*. It's flirty and fun and downright *wild*. Which means that the spanking would one-hundred percent turn into sex on the table I've been decorating for Christmas dinner with our friends…who will be here very soon.

Nope. Can't do it.

I step away from the table and squeeze my eyes closed. "They're shut. I promise."

He makes a disgruntled noise. "Little bird, I dare you to disobey me. Please?"

He sounds so pitiful that I *almost* give in. "My eyes are closed."

There's a dramatic sigh before I hear his bare feet pad closer. *And…bells?*

"What is that?" I ask, not daring to open my eyes.

He chuckles. "Beau and I went shopping during lunch the other day."

The idea of Pritch and his best friend, Beau, going on a shopping trip is almost comical. It has taken me some time to get used to Beau's stoic and standoffish nature. I think the moment I finally realized Beau wasn't as intimidating as he looks, was at his wedding to Jessa last month. He cried as Jessa read her vows, then could barely make it through his own. The secret is out: Beau Gamble is a softie.

But would he willingly go shopping with my eccentric husband? Doubtful. Half the time when the two are together, I'm surprised Beau doesn't murder him. Pritch is *exceedingly* good at finding a boundary, then needling at it.

"Okay, baby, here's your surprise," he says excitedly, followed by more jingles. The word *surprise* makes my heart thud a little. I have a surprise for him later, too, and I can't help worrying he won't be as thrilled about it as I am. "Open your eyes."

I do and…*wow.*

He's wearing a black sweater with white snowflakes, little red donkeys and one large donkey, which has a kiss mark on its butt. Words read, "Merry Kissmyassmas."

My attention quickly falls from his sweater to his…well, lack of clothing elsewhere. His legs are bare, accentuating a large, glittery red bow covering Pritch's penis. Or as he would call it—his best asset.

I open my mouth to say something, but nothing comes out.

"You're speechless. You love it!" My husband turns to the side, pointing. "Look, it's on a sock! I'm wearing a cock sock!"

"Did you buy this with Beau?" I ask, not sure why *that's* my question. But oh my gosh, poor Beau.

"Internet, thank you very much. That site where I buy our fun toys from." *Thank God.* "So, thoughts? Does this put you in the ho-ho-ho fucking spirit?"

"You're ruining the Christmas innocence," I point out.

He shrugs. "You know I like dirtying up my good girl."

"It's very…you." For some reason, like all things with Pritch, I find a tingle building between my legs. I shift, trying to give myself relief. Dear lord, what has this man done to me?

"Shit, now the sock doesn't fit as well," he says and my eyes flit to his face to find a heated gaze and a smirk. They lower again and I realize he's grown hard.

Okay, *harder.*

A knock comes at the door and my cheeks feel like they've been set aflame.

I rush toward him and give a little push. "Go put pants on!"

He doesn't budge. "You don't want others to see me. How territorial, little bird."

"Pritch," I plead.

He cackles and turns away from me. "Okay, okay." All I can do is stare at his sculpted bare butt. How did I get so lucky?

I wait until our bedroom door is closed before I approach the front door. When I open it, I'm thankful the first guests to arrive are Jessa and Beau. If Pritch makes another ostentatious appearance, at least they're used to it. All Pritch's friends are used to his brand of chaos, but Beau knows him the best because they used to live together.

Jessa is wearing a cute red sweater-dress paired with a

Santa hat and necklace with holiday lightbulbs. Beau, on the other hand, is wearing a red shirt that says, "Ain't no laws when you're drinking with Claus."

He notices my gaze and says in his usual gruff tone, "Pritch made me buy it."

I laugh and give Jessa a hug. "I heard about your shopping trip."

"I'm assuming Pritch's account was more joyous," Jessa says.

"Probably took artist liberties," Beau grumbles.

"And you probably compared the experience to a *Saw* movie," Pritch says, joining us. He presses a kiss to my temple. I glance quickly at his legs, thankful to see pants. He catches me and smirks, "No need to worry, I only show you the goods now."

My cheeks burn even hotter as I avoid Jessa and Beau's reactions. I could heat the oven *and* cook the Christmas ham with the heat from my cheeks.

"You're embarrassing your wife," Jessa points out.

"Say that again. Remind me this gorgeous woman belongs to me," Pritch says, deadly serious and reverent. My face cools. There are worse things than J.D. Pritchard being *completely* obsessed and in love with you. "Did you bring the booze?"

Beau glowers at him. "I'm not your personal bartender."

Pritch only shrugs.

"I've got all the ones you asked for in the car. Come help me."

Beau owns a bar in town, which the group of guys we're friends with frequent. Pritch used to spend a lot of his free time trying to numb his depression with alcohol. Since we've been married, he only drinks socially. He's been tickled pink trying to find cocktails for him—probably Beau—to make. Smoking Bishop and Hot Gin Punch are two he chose specifically because of *A Christmas Carol.*

"Oh my goodness, your tree is gorgeous!" Jessa squeals and moves closer to the nine-foot tree in our living room.

"My dad bought it for us," I tell her, thinking of when my dad told me he had bought it during the Christmas in July sale. He was so excited—Pritch jokingly said he seemed more thrilled about that than he did on the day of our wedding. Which we both know is impossible. Despite my dad being a preacher and Pritch's abundance of tattoos, piercings, and foul words, they get along well. In a way, my dad fills the empty places where Pritch's parents should be. "And I thrifted all of the ornaments."

"Wow, they're in such great condition." She touches one of my favorite hand-painted ones. "And the lights? Are they old, too?"

"Just made to look that way," I explain. "Pritch found them."

"He's so good to you," she says, looking at me with a wide grin. "I'm so thankful he has you."

"Me too, I don't know how I got so lucky."

The door opens again and Pritch walks in with an arm full of alcoholic bottles and nods to the other people following him. "Look who we found trespassing!"

"You invited us," Cain Hazelton grouses. Cain pretends to dislike Pritch, but he's also the first one to show up to help Pritch with home renovations. He's carrying a cake container in one hand, while his other arm is wrapped around his wife, Max, who happens to be eight months pregnant. I know they say pregnant women glow, but Max radiates in an angelic way. She's dressed in a cute, green maternity dress to match the plaid shirt her husband is wearing. They both have on a pair of elf-ear headbands, although on Max it's cute and on Cain it's downright comical.

Cain's best friend, Connor—who also happens to be Jessa's brother—follows in behind them with his wife, Erin, and daughter, Olivia. The little girl waves happily with her free hand, her other holding a basket of muffins. They're all in matching gnome pajamas.

"It smells amazing in here," Erin says, sniffing the air.

Olivia hands off the muffin basket and flings herself into Jessa's arms. They laugh and spin around.

"Pais has outdone herself," Pritch tells our friends, having set down the liquor bottles. He wraps his arms around my waist and buries his nose in the crook of my neck. "Ham, potatoes, green beans, something with Jello in it, biscuits that Dolly Parton would clutch her pearls over…hope you all brought your sweatpants."

***

"If I eat another bite, I'll be eighty-percent food and twenty-percent baby," Max says with a laugh as Cain motions toward his plate of desserts. "Paisley, everything was so delicious."

"Thank you," I say with a blush. It's high praise coming from Max, who owns the diner in town.

"So, what is everyone's plans for the holiday?" Pritch asks before stealing the final slice of cake. How does he eat so much, look so attractive, and *not* work out? Sometimes, I think he must be inhuman.

Cain and Max share a look; Max's eyebrows are raised, and Cain looks exceptionally grumpy. He's the one who answers first, surprisingly. "So close to the baby being due, we've asked family to come to us."

"He's afraid I'll go into labor," Max explains with a small laugh. "There are hospitals everywhere, you know?"

"Yeah, but we're prepared here," Cain explains, looking genuinely nervous.

Max lays her hand over his. "No matter what, our baby boy will be born happy and healthy, with the *best* daddy."

Cain grins.

"Have you settled on a name yet? Since Pritchard was shot down," Pritch asks pulling a glum face.

"I'm not naming my kid after you," Cain growls. He brings Max's hand to his lips before saying, "Ethan Rex Hazelton, but we'll call him Rex."

Erin makes a small noise, and we all look at her. There are tears in her eyes. "I already knew, but every time I hear it..." she trails off. I'm always unbelievably in awe of the ways Max honors her late-fiancé, Ethan, and Cain's unyielding support. Ethan was Erin's little brother. Erin manages to pull herself together, then continues, "We're spending Christmas Eve with Jessa and Beau, then we're heading to my parent's house. Ellie and Danny are coming into town, so it'll be a full house. What about you two?"

"Well, we've got custody of Jessa and Beau for Christmas Day. Paisley's dad is joining us for dinner, too," Pritch answers and I can't help but smile. Even if they don't act like it, he and Beau are practically brothers. When Jessa initially mentioned their plans with Erin's family, I could tell Pritch was disappointed; he didn't want to spend Christmas without Beau. It was Beau who piped up and said they didn't have any plans for Christmas Day. I think he wanted to spend the holiday with Pritch—his found family.

"This is my practice run," I tell them.

"Can't wait for the real thing," Beau says almost as happily as he sounds when talking about or to Jessa. I guess food is the way to his heart.

"And what is little miss Olivia getting for Christmas?" I ask.

Connor sighs. "Everything."

"Oh, you're the problem, you know. Spoiling her," Erin warns, kisses her husband's cheek.

"Dollhouse!" Olivia answers cheerfully, then frowns. "I asked for a brother or sister, but Mommy said that's up to her and Daddy, not Santa."

We all laugh and, surrounded by people I never expected to meet or love like family, in a life I didn't expect for myself, I feel thankful. Joyful. The coma I was in might have stalled my life, but it led me here. *To these people.*

***

Pritch cages me in against the counter, his lips brushes below my ear, as he murmurs, "Dishes can wait, little bird. I can't."

Suddenly, the air leaves my lungs, and my hands start to shake. It's now or never. I thought about waiting until Christmas to make the moment special, but I can't wait another few weeks. Not with the way my stomach turns every time I smell, see, or *think* about chicken. "I have something to give you first."

"Better than my—hey, what's wrong?" With his hands on my hips, he spins me around and searches my eyes. "Talk to me? Do you feel okay?"

"Yeah, it's just...you'll see."

I move away from him and walk toward our Christmas tree on unsteady legs. When I find the present I'm looking for, I close my eyes tight and hope he'll be happy. I turn around and instantly some of my anxiety fades when I find him practically glued to my back, anxiety furrowing his handsome features.

I hold the little box out to him and bite my lip. He takes it curiously—almost reverently—and slowly unties the sparkling red bow I spent at least a half-hour perfecting. "Did you do this?" he asks. When I nod, he shakes his head. "I feel bad undoing it." He slips the ribbon into his pocket, then takes off the lid of the box. As soon as he does, he goes completely still.

"Is this..."

I can't help but grin, my words failing me. Tears instantly fill my eyes. I desperately want him to be happy. I want him to be excited.

The decision to stop my birth control a few months ago wasn't a huge conversation, or even a huge moment. It was after we'd spent the day with Jessa and Beau while they watched Olivia. He just said, "Let's start a family."

I know how hard it was for him to say that and how hard it will be for him to wrap his mind around being a dad. Pritch has overcome so many obstacles when it comes to parents—first following his dad's suicide, then his mom's selfishness. It caused him to worry about his capacity to be a good dad. And I know, more than anything, he's worried about passing down his depression.

He lifts out the ultrasound photo and holds it close to his face. His thumb traces over it gently, but his expression is emotionless.

"I'm a little over six weeks along," I tell him in a slow, nervous voice. When he only continues to stare at the ultrasound, I ask, "Are you happy?"

He swallows and looks at me. "Am I happy?" The words seem foreign to him, like he doesn't know what I've asked. Then he releases a curse and says, "Yeah, I'm happy." The emotion still seems disconnected from him, but then his eyes turn glassy and single tear trails down his cheek. "I'm ecstatic."

I can't help myself—I throw my body against his. His arms go around me, the box falling to the floor. "We're going to be parents," I manage through my own tears.

He buries his face in my hair. "I love you, Pais. More than anything. And this baby...damn it, I'm at a loss for words for once."

I pull away from him and cover his cheeks with my hands, waiting for him to find the words.

"You're everything I never thought possible for myself," he finally manages. He looks away from my face for a split second, at the ultrasound photo. "I didn't dream of a life for myself before you. I didn't think I had anything to look forward to. But when I earned your love, I knew I was wrong. I started dreaming of *this*. Of a life with you—of a family with you." He pulls away and wipes at my tears. "I'm fucking terrified, though. That's okay, right?"

I laugh. "Yes, I am, too."

"But we've got this. We're going to be the best damn parents. This kid is going to be the luckiest little motherfu— when should I start censoring myself?"

"I think we're fine for now."

He lifts me up with an blissful smile. "Good because daddy has some dirty things to say to mommy."

He stops halfway to our bedroom and drops me back to my feet. His kisses me deeply to the point that when he pulls away, we both gasp for breath. "This is the best Christmas already, little bird, and the best present I've ever received."

Don't Miss the Rest of the LOVE IN MOTION series.

MOVING FORWARD

He's her anchor. She's his life preserver.

Maxine Dawson is pretending. She's pretending to be excited for her best friend's impending wedding, pretending her plans don't involve moving back in with her parents, pretending she can move on from her past. Mostly, she's been pretending that she's been okay since her fiancé, Ethan, died.

Cain Hazelton is many things, but he is not pretending. Everyone knows about his short fuse, his preference for seclusion, that he only lets himself care about one person - his Grams.

When Max and Cain's worlds collide, they gravitate toward each other for different reasons. For Max, Cain shuts down her constant flood of emotions and for Cain, Max makes him *feel* his emotions for the first time in his life. But before they can find their happiness they must overcome their pasts, their fears, and take a chance on love.

Liz Ashlee's stories are emotional reads about real world problems. Fans of An Optimist's Guide to Heartbreak/A

Pessimist's Guide to Heartbreak by Jennifer Hartmann and Ten Tiny Breaths by K.A. Tucker will love her romance about grief and finding the one who makes you want to live again.

Excerpt:

"Do you think the stars get lonely?" I ask in a whisper.

I expect him to ask if I'd had something to drink tonight. I'm already internally yelling at myself for saying that out loud. But he tilts his head back and follows my line of sight. "They're light-years apart and I know from experience that even being right next to someone can be lonely. But I think for a star it's a lot different." He pauses and turns his head slowly until his eyes are on me again. "I think stars glow brighter than any light in the world, and just being able to see another star—to know it's out there—is enough to soothe them. You beat loneliness by realizing there's a whole world out there, not just you."

I close my eyes and feel my lips tug into a smile. This man— he's slowly entering my heart. "You're a poet too."

He runs his hand through his hair and grips the back of his neck. "That's stretching it, Max."

"No, it isn't," I disagree. "That was probably one of the most beautiful things I've ever heard."

A slow, easy grin spreads across his lips, his eyes still lingering on me. My heart starts to pick up the slightest bit, sending shivers down my back. Knowing the rarity of those smiles, and that he's already given me so many tonight, makes me feel a little drunk. It's going to be my life's mission to see him smile, no matter how much that scares me.

COUNTING BACKWARD

She's his soulmate. He's her biggest regret.

Jessa Monroe is a survivor. She's survived heartbreak, a difficult childhood, and her mama's maniac boyfriend. What she isn't sure she can survive is Beau Gamble walking back into her life.

Beau left Jessa because he loved her. At the time, it was the only way to keep her safe. But when they reunite, he realizes he left her unprotected during the worst moment of her life.

All he can do is try to break through Jessa's walls so he can be with her again—back where he belongs. But Jessa can't trust that Beau won't walk away as he did once before. To protect her heart, she's built tall and strong walls around it. Beau is determined to prove he's here to stay and that he never stopped loving her. He knows that she is meant to be his first, last, and only love.

Liz Ashlee's stories are emotional reads about real world problems. Fans of The Problem with Forever *by Jennifer L. Armentrout and* All the Little Things *by Rachel Leigh will love her romance about grief and finding the one who makes you want to live again.*

Excerpt:

"Good morning, I'm—"

The husky voice slithers inside my chest and squeezes my heart, stopping it cold.

Jessa.

I've dreamed about her and tortured myself with memories of her for years because I've wanted to keep her with me—to grab hold of her before she disappeared right along with my soul. Her beauty, both inside and out, is almost transcendent—I always wondered how God could put someone so beautiful and kind on the earth when he could also create the most vile and corrupt people. Her long, deep brown hair looks just as soft as ever. My fingers are still itching to run through it. Her eyes are the same indescribable blue, shining bright, showing her every emotion, just as innocent and kind as the first day I let her into my life. And that freckle. . . the one on her chin that she always complained about . . . I loved that freckle and I made sure to tell her and show her just how much. God. I still love it. Still love her.

Her gaze flickers to mine and all of the love and warmth I've been starving for hits me like a concrete wall. As realization dawns on her, her eyes almost pulsate with it. More intense than ever, like that love never ended and grew into something more. Something stronger. Then, just as quickly, it disappears into horror and hatred. . . and *fear.* She lets out a strangled cry.

CRASHING SIDEWAYS

He's her dream man. She's his confessional.

J.D. Pritchard had no intention of stepping foot in Paisley Kelley's hospital room, let alone visiting her for the next three years. But once he starts, he can't stop.

When Paisley wakes up after her three-year coma, she remembers fragments of Pritch's one-sided conversations—but was he real or was that just her imagination running wild? It isn't until a chance meeting that she realizes the man of her dreams is a living, breathing, tattooed and *sexy* playboy.

None of the men in Pritch's family have lived passed their forties and he knows his time on Earth is limited. Except the more time he spends with Paisley, the more he realizes he can't push her away. He may not be able to promise her a lifetime of love, but he can promise to give her everything else.

The final book in the Love in Motion trilogy has all the feels you have come to love in a Liz Ashlee book—flawed characters, gripping storyline, and tempestuous love. The happily ever after will have fans of Asher by Carian Cole and Repeat by Kylie Scott falling in love with CRASHING SIDEWAYS.

Excerpt

The hairs stand up on the back of my neck.

I'm not alone.

I turn slowly to find a pair of haunting eyes staring back at me. One green, one blue, both vibrant. I've never seen someone with eyes like that—it's both unsettling and like a siren's call, beckoning me forward. But with sirens, there's always a shipwreck, isn't there? And this man... he screams peril ahead.

He's sitting on a half-wall, his back against the brick of the building. No, not sitting. Lounging. As if one false move won't send him falling toward the concrete two and a half stories below. There's a paperback resting on one thigh and a steaming mug on his other, held by a strong, tattooed hand. A blue star flower rests in the book, stem tucked away in the seam. His white-blond hair is cut short on the sides, and long on the top in a pompadour style, and he's wearing a leather jacket and jeans.

He's easily the most handsome man I've ever seen, but it's his mouth that takes me aback. His lips are turned up in a smirk, like he's caught his very own canary. That smile alone is something the older church ladies would likely deem sinful. It's definitely... devilish.

He's all confidence and charisma.

"S-sorry, I didn't realize anyone was out here," I manage.

His eyes become hooded as his gaze roams over me. No one—not even Cameron—has ever looked at me so closely that it feels as if my blood will boil in my veins. I'm not dressed like any of the other girls at the party. Not just because some of them are showing a lot of skin, but they're fashionable. Me? I settled for my usual style, which looks as if I was peeled off the cover of a 1950s cookbook. I'm wearing a short-sleeved cream sweater tucked into a pair of high-waisted, teal corduroy capris. I've even got a headband on. I belong in a supermarket searching the aisles for cream of mushroom and Jell-O, not here.

"I'm willing to share my balcony of solitude with a lady in need," he tells me in a voice that rolls over me like the sunrise on a chilly morning. Warm. Comforting. It takes on a rumbling tone as he murmurs, "Little bird."

My heart tumbles in my chest. That voice.

This is the man from my dreams.

AVAILABLE IN EBOOK AND PRINT WHERE BOOKS ARE SOLD.

ABOUT THE AUTHOR

Liz Ashlee is a romance novelist known for the Love in Motion series, Sort of Normal, Step Toward You and Heart's a Mess. Liz has her M.A. in English from Northern Kentucky University, where she also earned her undergraduate degrees. Liz lives in Kentucky with her husband, son, and their plethora of pets.

Facebook: https://www.facebook.com/LizAshleeAuthor
Instagram: https://www.instagram.com/lizashleeauthor/
TikTok: https://www.tiktok.com/@liz.ashlee
Goodreads: https://www.goodreads.com/author/show/17742563.Liz_Ashlee
BookBub: https://www.bookbub.com/profile/liz-ashlee
Website: https://www.liz-ashlee.com/

As Shadows Lengthen

A Shadows of Roots and Wings origin Short

By A. D. Brazeau

As Shadows Lengthen

Nathan

I stood at my open locker, waiting for Everly. All I wanted to do was go home and work on my history paper, but something told me to wait for her. Everly hadn't been herself lately, or maybe ever, if I was being totally honest. There always seemed to be something hanging over her head. If I were into the spooky stuff like she and Rose were, I might think Everly was haunted.

Everly rounded the corner, practically dragging her backpack behind her, and for one mad second, I contemplated dropping my stuff and scooping her up in my arms. She looked that bad.

"Everly, are you sick?" I felt my brows knit together as I held out a hand toward her. "Do we need to get you a stretcher?"

"Funny." She batted away my hand. "Just tired and weirded out. Rose made me sneak out last night and break into Red Manor. I can't believe you haven't heard. I would have thought that collapsing during class would immediately have been broadcasted all over school."

"Wait." I tried not to shake my head. Rose was always trying to one-up herself in terms of getting in trouble, and for some reason she felt the need to drag Everly along. "You two broke into Red Manor? And you collapsed during class? Start with that first. Are you okay?"

"I'm fine. Just embarrassed. I thought I saw something and felt faint, but my exhausted brain was playing tricks on me."

She didn't look too convinced of her own words, even as she said them. Everly often thought she was seeing things. Fletcher told me in private, and on more than one occasion, that he thought she was schizophrenic.

"What happened at Red Manor?" I shifted uncomfortably on my feet. Red Manor was off limits to just about everyone. "Did you guys get caught?"

"Yeah, although I don't remember it. I had gotten a little spooked, then hit my head so hard on the door that I blacked out. Apparently the noises we heard that scared me were just the mayor working late."

I swiped a hand through my hair as I tried to process everything Everly was saying. "You knocked yourself out? That's probably why you thought you were seeing things in class. You have a concussion. You should be sleeping." As captain of the football team, I knew a thing or two about concussions, and if what Everly said was true, she should be home resting.

"I'm fine." Everly shouldered her backpack in typical stubborn style. She couldn't admit defeat to anyone.

I just shook my head. "Did you get in trouble?"

She shrugged. "A little, I guess."

All I could do was shake my head again. "You two should cool it with the antics."

"*Okay, Dad.*" Everly playfully kicked the toe of my shoe with hers. "Let's talk about something else. Like, don't you have practice?"

I turned from her, shoving my physics book into my locker. I pulled out my backpack and slammed the door.

The paper skeleton taped to the outside of my locker fluttered, his bony hand drooping in a sad wave. I thought about last Halloween and how much fun we'd all had, each of us dressed as members of a pirate crew. This year felt less innocent, adulthood looming large over each of us. I had to wonder if we'd do anything fun for Halloween, or if Rose would make us sit around the cemetery, a Ouija board spread on the grass. I preferred costumes and candy to the scent of rot.

I faced Everly. "Cancelled. Half the team has the flu, which is what I thought you had the second I saw you dragging ass down the hall." I shouldered my pack. "I still can't believe you guys did that. Have you lost your mind, Everly? Rose is going to get you in serious trouble." I rolled my eyes like a disappointed parent. Getting in trouble was not my thing. My life was mapped. It started with football and school and ended with me as a famous historian.

"Probably, but it's fun, and Rose just needs it. *You know why*. She craves escape, I guess. Except for last night," Everly paused as we made our way down the hall, then continued, "our middle-of-the-night excursions are usually a blast. Rose had to blow off some steam. There was just something that made last night a little different."

"What do you mean?" I braced myself for more of Everly's paranormal obsessiveness. I could feel it coming. I didn't think she was crazy like Fletcher believed, but I wished she would move away from this stuff.

"I don't know. A *feeling*, something I couldn't explain. I saw something, I'm sure of it. An apparition, if that was what it was. I felt different the second I ran out of Red Manor."

I didn't want to get into it. I felt for Everly, and for Rose, whose home life was the worst, but I'd about had enough of the ghost stuff. We pushed our way through the exterior door, sunlight blinding us as we walked outside.

"I know Rose has it rough, but you have a shot at a full ride, wherever you want to go. Don't fuck that up. End of lecture." I was used to lectures, as that was the only way my parents knew how to communicate.

We lived about six blocks from school, next-door neighbors since birth. It was nice to walk with Everly, as long as I could get her onto other topics of conversation. I pointed out the fun Halloween decorations of our neighbors as we passed each house along the way. Our street really did it up for Halloween. Not a single house was sitting out the approaching holiday. There were witches brewing potions on lawns, giant spiders hanging off roofs, and jack-o-lanterns of every size, all intricately carved, leading up to every door.

We were about halfway home when Everly brought up something she and Rose were tentatively calling *Murder Club*.

"I know you get annoyed with the paranormal stuff, but this is different. Less ghosty, more paranormal. It'll be fun. You, me, Rose, Fletch, and Leigh, that new girl Anna. Maybe Jonathan, I haven't decided yet."

Everly glanced toward the road, but not before I caught a faint blush on her cheek. I grunted. "If everyone else is in, I guess I am, too."

I thought Everly would be excited, but she abruptly stopped walking and reached out a desperate hand for me. Her knees collapsed, and she went down hard on the pavement. Everything happened so fast, there was no time to be scared. I dropped my backpack and crouched down next to Everly. I asked her over and over if she was okay until I was yelling in her ear, my breath all but stopped, my heart in my throat.

I put a hand on her chest. Her heartbeat felt ragged. I had no idea what that meant.

"What the hell, Everly? Are you okay? I'm calling for help." I was about to start screaming for help when she squeezed my arm.

"No, don't," She gasped, gulping down air. "I'm okay."

Was this all from last night's concussion? She looked more tired than I'd ever seen her in my life, even more so than the time she'd had pneumonia in elementary school. Maybe she was coming down with the flu, like the football team, on top of the concussion.

The air around us went ice cold. Everly flinched so hard to the side that her small body slammed into my large one. "Did you see that? There's a dark haze in the corner of my right eye."

"What? Everly, you're scaring me. Let me run to the house and call 911."

"No," She grabbed my other hand with her free one. "I'm okay. I must be getting that flu or something. You should keep your distance."

She pushed off me, regaining her wobbly legs. They shook with the effort to stand, but I held onto her even though she tried to do it on her own.

I didn't keep my distance. Instead, I grasped her arm the rest of the way home. I left Everly at the door of her house with explicit instructions to call me if she started to feel worse. "At the very least, call your mom, and you need to go to bed," I said.

I knew she wasn't about to call her mom, but I hoped she would at least sleep. I wasn't going to think about the cold I had felt. There must be a very logical explanation. The cold was because I was getting sick, like everyone else. *End of story.* Everly and her hallucinations were just that. *Hallucinations.* It had nothing to do with whatever she thought she saw last night.

***

Everly

By seven o'clock the next night, Rose and I were fluffing floor pillows and setting out drinks for the *Murder Club*. "You're not, like, contagious anymore, right?"

The crow's nest had always been my favorite place. As a little kid, I would bring my dolls up and stage elaborate scenes, using the entirety of the four-sided, box-like room as my dollhouse. There were 360-degree views from which I could see almost all of my neighborhood, including Nathan's bedroom window, where he would often leave messages for me taped to the glass.

Later, I made the crow's nest my reading and hangout room, with a bookshelf I'd rescued from the curb and painted white, and a small table in the corner for my mom's old record player. During the day, it was flooded with light, and at night, there was no better place for relaxation with the soft light from the streetlight out front and the bright stars overhead. The views of the neighborhood afforded a little spying action that Rose couldn't get enough of.

I fluffed my last pillow, spun around, and dropped onto the small, decades-old couch, pushed up against the west wall. "Rose, come on. We both know I wasn't actually sick. I whacked the hell out of my head, and I think," I paused, unsure of how to express to Rose what I had suspected all along. "I think, maybe, that thing, whatever it was we saw, is haunting me." I knew it sounded ridiculous the second it was out of my mouth, but there was not another human on the face of the earth whom I could confide in like this. My mom would think I was nuts and send me to counseling, or worse, to the school counselor, and Nathan hadn't seemed like he'd really wanted to talk about it.

Rose took a long drink of her Dr. Pepper, her gaze on me the whole time. "Babes, it wasn't a ghost, and even if it was, ghosts don't just leave the places they haunt. I don't think they can, they're like stuck there, or something. Besides freaking out in first period, what else makes you say that?" She leaned against the east windowsill.

"What I didn't tell you is that I saw something hazy in the corner of my eye. That's what startled me in class. I saw the same thing walking home with Nate and almost passed out. I've seen it three more times since then, and I always feel cold when it appears." I bit my lip. I felt like I was rambling, but the look on Rose's face told me she thought

I was freaking out over nothing. "And then there's the nightmares. I've been having nightmares all week and haven't been able to sleep. Every time I close my eyes, I wake up in the dream, and there's just this heavy, earthy darkness all around me. I'm strapped to a chair and there's blood on my arm."

Rose dropped next to me and patted my knee like she was a parent consoling a distraught child. "Babes, we have several things to unpack here. The first is that you never sleep, and you always have nightmares. This is nothing new, so don't blame the poor ghost of Red Manor."

"Don't call it that," I groaned.

"I wasn't finished." Another pat on the knee. "It wasn't a ghost, *Ever*. Seriously, it wasn't. I would bet you a hundred dollars it was those old creeps who hang out there. They were messing with us. What I think is so fascinating about you, my friend, is that you will pee your pants over a supposed ghost but have no problem with being a member of this little crime club."

"I'm not peeing my pants. I've handled it quite well, thank you." It was true. I hadn't once tried to slip into my mom's bed. I was too old for that. "And I'm not in love with the idea of this club. You know I don't like this stuff like you do. I am just enjoy humoring you." I made a face and stuck out my tongue.

It was mostly true. Although marginally interested in true crime, I was doing this for Rose. Her home life was as bad as it got, and if she needed to start a club in my crow's nest, then I was going to give it to her. There would be another time to revisit what happened at Red Manor, to dive into what was happening to me. My moment would come, it just wasn't now.

Don't Miss the Rest of the Mystery...

IN THE SHADOWS OF ROOTS AND WINGS

Everly Palmer swore she'd never return to Splendid, Colorado—a town too perfect to be real and too haunted to forget. But when news of a childhood friend's sudden death reaches her, she's drawn back to this unusual place. Founded by her ancestor, Splendid is a town frozen in time, its beauty unmarred, its secrets buried deep. Everly has spent her life trying to decipher the cryptic nightmares that plague her, and now, back in the town she once fled, she begins to suspect they were never just dreams.

As the funeral passes and the shadows lengthen, Everly stumbles upon a forgotten grave and a chilling truth: Splendid's perfection is not a gift, but a curse. Old ties with her estranged friend Rose fray under the weight of buried memories and sinister revelations. The deeper Everly digs, the more she realizes Splendid was never meant to be escaped. In a town where nature doesn't obey natural law and happiness comes at a terrible cost, Everly must choose—unearth the truth and risk being swallowed whole or surrender to the darkness that's waited for her return.

In the Shadow of Roots and Wings is a suspenseful mystery that meets magical realism, reminiscent of *The Secret History* by Donna Tartt and *The Maidens* by Alex Michaelides, and is set in the fictional town of Splendid, Colorado.

Author A. D. Brazeau's latest mystery grips readers on the first page and never lets go.

Excerpt-

Everly strode toward the back of the cemetery, to the section she knew was the oldest. The markers here were more prominent, some tall obelisks, some giant slabs of granite or marble. Most were so old that the names and epitaphs were faded, barely legible in some places. She'd never been that far in, but something propelled her away from the funeral, in the direction opposite her car. The farther she walked, the quieter it was.

A tall gravestone, the likes of which she'd never seen, caught her eye. She moved toward what appeared to be a cylindrical column. As she drew closer, she realized the column was a tree trunk.

"Wow." She ran her hand over what felt like plaster, spread on the piece in a way that made it look like real bark. A few branches jutted off at various angles, adding to the naturalistic effect. A symbol was etched below the epitaph.

She pulled her reading glasses out of her vintage handbag, then knelt on the ground. She'd seen Mason's symbols on graves many times, but never had she seen anything like this. This was a figure eight, the symbol for infinity, lying on its side. Inside one loop was a wing, and inside the other was a tree with exposed roots. She ran her finger over and around the loops. There was something familiar about the symbol, but she couldn't say what.

Unusual, for sure.

She stood, pulling out her phone to snap a photo of the grave. If anything, this may be fun to investigate, to give her something to do while she was in Splendid. Standing back to line up her picture, she spied another tree trunk-like grave not far off.

"What in the world?"

She captured her picture, then took off for the second grave.

"Everly." The deep, smoky voice that called out was unmistakable.

I should have gone to my car. Why hadn't she done that?

Everly turned her heel in the grass. "Hi, Rose."

There was a glare behind Rose. The sun streaming through tree limbs framed her in goddess-like light. She stood before Everly in her designer dress, her sky-high heels in one hand. They were probably too expensive to get dirty.

Everly was right about one thing: Rose hadn't aged a day. Even up close, she'd barely changed. Matured, maybe, her face a little slimmer in the cheeks, but all in all, she looked the same.

Rose wasn't alone. Fletcher and Leigh, hand in hand as always, walked up behind her.

Rose glanced over her shoulder at them momentarily, then directed her attention back at Everly. "We were surprised to see you here. Pleasantly surprised."

The sentiment took Everly a little aback. She needed a second to compose her thoughts and make sure she didn't say anything stupid, but then matched Rose's honesty with her own. "I surprised myself. Mom told me what happened last week, but I didn't decide to come until this morning. A last-minute plane ticket meant a back-row seat."

"Sitting by the bathrooms is the worst." Rose looked Everly up and down. "You look great, Ever. You've hardly changed."

Everly blinked in surprise. Not only had Rose been friendly so far, but she'd used the nickname she'd given her in preschool. Before Everly could respond, Leigh moved up alongside Rose.

"Hardly a wrinkle," Leigh said. "And the same chestnut hair I always envied. Now, I'd take some hair. Any kind."

Leigh touched the edge of her blue head scarf. Her once bright blue eyes were dull and bloodshot, the skin around them sunken and dark.

Discomfort edged around Everly's gut as her mind scrambled for something to say. She ran a hand through her hair, then felt like maybe that was showing off. She wanted to throw up. Social interactions had never been her strong suit. "It's dyed these days. There are so many grays, I'm considering letting it go."

How do you ask a former best friend about her apparent illness? Was it rude to ask, or was it rude not to ask? If only someone would speak and save her from this moment.

Everly glanced over at Fletcher, who was staring off into space. He looked like his dad had when they were in school, except Fletcher was more fit. His hair was more gray than black, his face smooth, except for two deep parentheses lines on either side of his mouth, and the crinkles around his eyes.

Rose cleared her throat. "Well, how long are you staying?"

Everly shrugged, grateful that the spell of awkwardness had been broken. She shifted her feet. God, they hurt. "Not sure. I don't have a return flight, so I might stay for a few days. I haven't seen my mom in years."

"Of course you haven't." Leave it to Rose to get in one good shot.

"Yeah, well, I'll see you guys around." Everly took off toward the parking lot. Drawing this out any longer was pointless. She heard Leigh say something behind her, but Everly was already twenty feet away, and there was no way she was turning around.

She flung off the too-tight pumps as she marched through the grass, past tombstone after tombstone, not bothering to retrieve them. They didn't fit anyway, kind of like her.

AVAILABLE WHERE BOOKS ARE SOLD.

ABOUT THE AUTHOR

A.D. Brazeau is an award-winning author who writes what she loves. From dark and fantastical fairytale retellings to quirky romance and everything in between, she loves nothing more than to immerse herself in new worlds. A.D. Brazeau is a book-obsessed wife, mother, and dog lover who grew up surrounded by stories. Not much has changed. A.D. is from Colorado Springs, CO.

'Ho-No

(A Tuckahoe Inn series short)

By Laurel Houck

CHAPTER ONE

"He's dead."

"Well, *do something.*"

The EMT guy stares at me. "I'm not a miracle worker."

I shove him away from Barrington's motionless body and begin to push against the hairy, pale-white chest I know so well. Thank goodness I took a CPR class at the Club. With each compression, the mattress moans beneath him— much like he had been moaning only moments before. I know my silk dressing gown is gaping open as my boobs bounce up and down in rhythm with my hands. The EMT's eyes follow their journey. I still have it, even if it's drooping ever so slightly these days.

My mind drifts away to an hour ago. Barry and I, exchanging glances over champagne, strawberries, and eggs Benedict. My foot under the table, nudging the downy warmth between his widespread legs. His patented Ivy League grin as he handed me a box containing my Christmas present, a diamond necklace—not more than two carats and there may be a small inclusion, but still. He earned my enthusiastic appreciation under the covers.

It took me a minute to realize something had gone

wrong since being sweaty and out of breath was de rigueur during our trysts. The pale, gray skin and retching, highly unusual, brought an end to everything. Including, apparently, Barrington.

"Lana Morrissey?" I look up into a new face. Hard eyes stare at me from under a black cap with a gold insignia on the front. "Abe Sargent, Capitol Police Sargent. The paramedics assure me that Congressman Montgomery is beyond your help."

I continue to press on Barry's chest, even as a giggle rises in my throat. "Do they call you Sargent Sargent?"

He grabs my hands, grazing my breast in the process, and stops my movement. "I'm very sorry. Your…friend…is gone."

"Really?" I wrench away from his vice grip. "He's right here. Not gone. Nope. You're wrong."

But as his words smack me upside the face, I realize they're true. Barry, *my Barry*, is dead. That last moan…climax of our final tête-à-tête or final climax of his life? I feel hot tears pushing against my eyelids. Questions tumble through my brain, unraveling like a ball of yarn. *Did I love him, was he using me, what about his wife, will I miss him?* But overriding each come the much more important, big kahuna questions: *What will I do now? What will happen to me?*

"Get dressed." Sargent Sargent steps back as I climb down from the four-poster bed. Barry did have excellent taste in the furnishings he bought for me. "Then we talk."

I gather my robe around me, and with the dignity befitting the mistress of a five-term member of Congress, march to my dressing room. Although I want to puke, *what the hell will happen to me*, I duck into the ensuite. After a quick shower—really, poor dead Barry did sweat a lot under the sheets even in the best of times—I choose a casual, yet tasteful, outfit. It is the holidays after all, tragedy notwithstanding. Black slacks and a cashmere sweater from Saks with a sparkling sequined Christmas tree on the front. Black, low-heeled Ferragamo pumps, so last-season but serviceable for the occasion. The new diamond necklace clasps around my long neck. I add diamond earrings that returned with my lover from a government fact-finding mission two years ago to Botswana. They are of questionable provenance, but I have no time to get the good ones from the safe.

Pulling my hair into a neat chignon with an added sprig of faux mistletoe to try and capture at least a scintilla of holiday spirit, I pass through the bedroom into the living room. The white carpet whispers under the leather soles of my shoes. That familiar sound is overtaken by squeaky wheels. A gurney carrying a black bag is whisked past me, shearing off a fragrant pine branch and setting a bell ringing on the Christmas tree.

"'Every time a bell rings, an angel gets his wings.'" No one else seems to notice. "It's the famous line from the beloved Frank Capra classic Christmas film, It's a Wonderful Life. Barry and I saw it at the Avalon cinema just last week. And now…"

No one responds to my poignant statement, boorish Neanderthals. They enter the elevator at the end of the room. As the doors whoosh closed, I know this will be the last time Barrington graces my penthouse. He leaves black wheel marks on the rug.

"Sit down." Abe gestures to the pale blue silk sofa. "Please."

I bend my knees, noticing not for the first time that they're creaking, and lower my 'tight ass', Barry's parting compliment to me, onto the cushion. "I'm in no mood to discuss this business right now. It's much too…distressing." It's not hard to release one tear down my right cheek. Practice makes perfect. I might even feel sad.

"What was your relationship with Senator Montgomery?"

"May I call you Abe?" I produce a wan smile that showcases my dimple.

He nods.

"The Senator and I were friends. *Close* friends."

"Did you have a relationship of a sexual nature?"

"You're the detective. Do you really think I was taking dictation in bed?" Sad smile number two. "I'm so sorry. Yes, we were discussing marriage. So, of course, that led to a certain degree of intimacy."

"Was Mrs. Montgomery aware of any of this?"

Bitch. Her sour disposition couldn't be sweetened no matter what Barry said or did. "I believe so. He planned to leave her after the next election cycle, which would have been his last."

"Uh huh. Right." Abe struggles not to roll his eyes. They stop halfway, making him appear demented. "Maybe he wasn't leaving her, and you resented the hell out of it."

Prove it stays unsaid. I dab at my eyes with one of Barry's monogrammed Egyptian cotton handkerchiefs. "He made me happy. No matter what our official relationship."

"There will be an autopsy. To rule out foul play." Abe looms over me. "Anything you'd like to share now, while I'm feeling some Christmas cheer?"

"Are you accusing me of a crime of passion? I assure you there is no crime here." I stand and glare up at the cop. Moistening my lips and adjusting my hips I add, "If it's passion alone you're looking for, look no further."

Abe snorts. "Yeah, okay Ms. Hot-to-Trot. I prefer my babes under fifty. No offense." He strides past the Christmas tree without a single compliment on the designer theme I chose this year, Silver Bells and Snowflake Bows.

A stab of unease moves through me. He's right. I'm getting...older. It takes time to develop a relationship to the point where one is housed in a penthouse, all bills paid, and diamond jewelry (even if it is white gold instead of platinum), with the breakfast cart.

"Condolences. Don't leave DC." Abe nods as the elevator doors close.

I need to call someone. But who? I lost track of most of my friends from my high-end call girl days when Barry made me his exclusive. And the ones before that, when I began working the streets, well, most are dead. I wonder what happened to Meadow? I ran into her a few years ago when I accompanied Barrington to a political rally in Pittsburgh. There she stood in Market Square, just another aging hippie who worked for too long in the world's oldest profession. She said she had a decent place to live, we exchanged phone numbers and never connected again.

I find her in my Contacts, tap the number, and hold my breath.

A hacking cough, remnant of too many joints, precedes, "Peace." I don't recognize the voice.

"Meadow? It's Lana Morrisey."

"Groovy." Another cough comes through the phone. "Not buying any crap, won't give you my social security number, got no credit cards. And there's no shitty meadow here."

"Oh." My predicament slams into my brain, including the need to get out of Washington for good. Barry protected me. His family will be a bitch to deal with after the way he died. This sounds like an old lady, one who hasn't aged well. Surely not *my* Meadow. Good breeding mandates a reply. "Sorry. Wrong number."

There's silence on the line, then, "Whatever."

I hear the strains of *In A Gadda Da Vida* in the background. Meadow liked Iron Butterfly too.

"Well, thank you." I want to hang up, but for some reason my finger lingers just above the red End.

"Not enough to do around here anyway. Glad to have a nice little chatty chat, as long as you aren't peddling life insurance." The stranger seems reluctant to end things, too. "This retirement home sucks. But the cake is good. Not like my brownies," she giggles, "but edible."

"You live in a nursing home?" I flick a piece of lint off my cashmere. I need a place to stay, but I'm not sick or old enough for a care facility.

"No!" Indignation floods the phone. "Independent

Living, asshole. F-you." The woman snorts and hangs up.

So, Meadow has changed phone numbers. Unless that was her, and she doesn't remember me. She might live in a commune, but would never be in a nursing facility. Who else can I call? I have no idea how to reach Carlene or if she'd even take my call after…everything. What to do, what to do?

The next seven days pass in a blur of waking nightmares. The official report, that Barry had a massive heart attack, frees me from guilt but not from total responsibility. As his daughter put it, 'Humping a whore killed my father no matter what the paperwork says.' Really, whatever happened to class? Barry must be rolling over in his grave. And missing his 'whore,' who understood him better than his own family.

The horrific week ends with Mr. Richard, the formerly ingratiating building manager, informing me to vacate the premises. As I spend Christmas day packing it becomes clear that four and a-half years of gyrating under Barrington, who never once let me be on top, has earned me very little in tangible assets for now. Hopefully the stock portfolio he set up for me will prove worthwhile. My jewelry and clothing fit into three Bottega Veneta bags. I shrug into my bobcat and fox jacket, pull on brown leather gloves, and let the doorman hail a cab and stow my luggage.

After the hour flight to Pittsburgh International Airport—which looks like a ghost town compared to Dulles—I take an Uber to the cheapest motel I could find on-line. City View Suites is a euphemism for a run-down fleabag of a place where it has to be more common to rent by the hour rather than by the night. How very annoying to fall so far, so fast. But with my tenuous financial situation, I can't afford to squander too much capital. There are affairs to be settled so that I get what's coming to me. Until then, prudent is the word du jour. I plan to end up on top. Unlike my boudoir experience with Barry.

After Lysoling the toilet, checking the bed for bugs, and making a cup of in-room tea that tastes like coffee since the appliance is stained brown, I sit at the tiny table. The red, dog-eared envelope from my purse has Carlene's return address:

Carlene Horst
69 Freestyle Road
Intercourse, PA 17534

Trust her to live in a town with that name. She's had plenty of experience with it. We all have. I permit myself a moment of grief for Barry, tinged with pride. When I met him, he went from a limp piece of bacon to a flaming sausage, sans little blue pill. It's a gift. One that I may be aging out of—but enough whining. It won't get me anywhere.

I can picture Carlene in the signature cowgirl outfit she favored, almost hear her West Texas accent that she exaggerated to make her stand out from the rest of us on Penn Avenue. Those were the days. Awake all night, fighting over johns, but protecting one another, sharing cigarettes. A tough life, without a doubt—sex work being illegal in Pennsylvania—but somehow a simpler time. We were young, beautiful, and ambitious.

And now? Old, worn, and wondering how and where to retire. Because although I know I've aged well and few would guess that there's more years behind me than in front of me, I suspect my career shelf life has been reached.

On my laptop I do a reverse search and come up with Carlene's phone number. It takes me a minute to still my heart. We were close once upon a time. Until it all changed. I close my eyes, whisper a quick expletive, and enter the number.

Just shoot me.

Don't Miss More Fabulous Reads by Laurel Houck

THE GIRL WITH CHAMELEON EYES

It's an abrupt, uncomfortable incarnation for Summer, the ghostly girl with chameleon eyes. Exotic hues roil in her gaze as she seeks to recall what awful sin in her past has doomed her to roam the earth. And to discover what—or who—will bring her to eternal rest.

Kota, brunt of bad jokes because he's different, feels an instant connection to Summer. She recoils at the mere sight of him. Yet they are drawn together in a dance of mutual need, choreographed by the ages.

As Summer grows more attached to both her young foster brother and to Kota's friend, Preston, she struggles against complacency. Until discovering that if she doesn't expiate the guilt on her soul by her seventeenth birthday, she will roam forever.

For her, it's hate at first sight. For him, it's instant attraction. When the pieces of their lives begin to unravel and intertwine, will love be enough to save them both? Or will evil decide their future?

EXCERPT-

My vapor solidifies with no warning whatsoever. Abrupt. Compact. Unexpected.

I'm near a dumpster that squats behind a floodlit Sheetz gas station, the stench of hot dog grease and burnt coffee strong in my nostrils. My feet are last to materialize, so that for a moment when I look down, I'm floating about five inches above the pavement, white mist above black asphalt.

With the physical transformation comes the rest of it. Light and cool converts to heavy and hot. Yearning and searching morphs to fear and uncertainty. Naked and misty transforms to flesh-bound and clothed. I'm grateful for the garments that cover my skin, even if how that happens is a mystery to me.

The nausea and dizziness are stronger than the last time I can recall. I lean against the dumpster and slide to the ground, knees up, head in my hands. It will pass soon. I hope.

"Miss, are you okay?" A deep voice rumbles above the traffic noise. The tall, ruddy-faced cop is standing over me, wearing a black uniform and a hat with a band of navy and gold squares. "I'm Officer Sullivan. Did someone hurt you?"

"I'm fine." I scramble to my feet, glad it's dim in the shadow of the dumpster. I'm still shaky and have no clue what color has risen in my eyes. Between the lights and my startling arrival, anything is possible.

I keep my head down. What can I tell him? I know that I used to be alive, that now I'm a ghost, and that I'm searching for something to expiate my guilt over...what? Beyond that, fuzzy at best.

LOVE IS A RIVER

Love dies with Abby's father. The return of her mother after a twelve-year absence brings more grief. And the move to a dilapidated house along the Youghiogheny River bike trail is an exile.

When blond, blue-eyed Jack rides into Abby's life, it's like the sun has been restored to her world. Bit by bit, hints of a darker side to his personality appear. She struggles to deny them, even while her best friend, Morton, grows increasingly mistrustful of the handsome stranger.

Abby uncovers a mystery from the Civil War era in a nearby cemetery, which brings her only moments of peace. Cool caresses and the whispered call, "Abigail..." send her digging into the past.

But as Jack's motives become ever more unclear, the love Abby hoped for seems impossible. And leads her to a life or death choice. Will love be her salvation ... or her demise?

EXCERPT-

A floorboard creaked over her head, and she stopped, her senses on high alert. Ghosts? Serial killer? She pressed her fingertips against the rough plaster wall, her ears tuned into every nuance of sound, her eyes scanning the stairwell.

Stale air clogged her lungs, and the metallic taste of fear drenched her mouth. She had read about murdered girls in abandoned houses. Thick old walls didn't let screams—or people—escape.

A door squeaked, a slow, deliberate sound followed by a stealthy footstep.

Abby waited in the curve of the stairs, back pressed against the wall. Her thin black sweater clung to her suddenly damp skin, and the urge to pee made her squirm. Footsteps came closer. She sniffed a sudden whiff of chocolate. The hair on her arms stood straight up, threaded between the goose bumps raised there. Her heart labored harder, a painful drumbeat in her chest. A dust mote floated through the air, tickling her nose with the threat of a sneeze. She held her breath, fight or flight vying for her attention. But if she didn't handle this, Lisa might get hurt, too.

Taking a deep breath, she peered around the corner.

A piercing shriek split her eardrums. "Ahhhhh."

SEARCHING FOR HOME

Life on the streets is hard but it's deadly when a young woman battles addiction...

Where is home...when you're homeless?

Selah gets through life using lies, sex, and faux concern as a veneer to forget the past and to achieve personal gain. She barely tolerates her job bringing medicine to the streets. Will is the only man who has refused her body. She resents that his God stands between them.

Will pastors the homeless no matter who or where they are. He conceals a past that is anything but pure. His biggest temptation is his love for Selah. But he refuses to compromise his faith.

When Selah's deceased husband appears to her—more dangerous in death than in life—the careful control she has used to cope slips away. Evil takes control as she falls far from the life she had carefully planned. And then farther still.

Selah must make a radical choice as an epic spiritual battle rages. Because she has finally found a love worth protecting at all costs.

Is there redemption at the intersection of brutal reality and saving grace?

Searching For Home is a gripping and too-real tale of love, addiction, and redemption; written by the one woman, Laurel Houck, who has championed salvation for hundreds of people. This amazing tale will have you brushing tears from your cheeks and will show you a hidden world our eyes have skipped over as we travel through big cities and small. Fans of realistic fiction like *Ruby (Between the Cracks, #1)* by P.D. Workman and *Broke(n)* by S.T. Jones will love Searching for Home.

All proceeds from the sale of this book will benefit homeless outreach, Light In My City,

www.lightinmycity.org

EXCERPT-

I don't give a crap about your name came to Selah's mind, but she managed a smile. "God help me, that's why I asked. But you don't have to tell me."

He shrugged and pulled up one sleeve to display a crude tattoo of a wrench. "Torque." After surveying her for a moment he added, "Do you always ask God to help you? And does he?"

"Just a figure of speech. No real meaning. I always refer God questions to the pastor over there." She gestured toward Will; his arms loaded with a stack of take-out boxes he added to a pile already on a bench beside his SUV. "Let's get you something to eat."

"Cool." Torque touched Selah's hand. "Thanks.

Selah pulled back from him.

"Oh, got it. No touching."

"It's just…" Selah reached out and clasped his hand with a firm grasp.

Her palm tingled, a mixture of fire and ice that shot tremors up her arm. She wanted to let go but she couldn't. Her eyes focused on his fingernails, encrusted with dirt and grease, red lesions on his knuckles—scabies perhaps—and frayed cuffs of a flannel shirt peeking out from under the sleeves of a dirty brown Carhartt jacket.

The sight, familiar. The feeling, unknown. Electric. But not sexual. How was that even possible?

Torque let go first. "I'm hungry."

"Oh. Of course. Follow me." They walked together toward the packaged meals. "How old are you?"

"Want to guess?" Torque stopped and gestured up and down his six-plus feet.

Selah figured he wouldn't be honest, but took a shot. "Eighteen?"

"Close enough."

Which meant he might be younger and not want to get involved with juvenile agencies. In spite of his strength and appearance, he didn't seem all that ready for street life. "Maybe we can get you connected to some people. Help you find your way home."

AVAILABLE IN EBOOK AND PRINT WHERE BOOKS ARE SOLD.

ABOUT THE AUTHOR

Laurel has traveled the road of writing since, at the age of six, she penciled her first book, Crawls the Caterpillar. With stops along the way for newspaper and magazine articles, she has published two Young Adult paranormal romance novels, one adult paranormal romance novel, and one Christian Devotional of original poetry. She loves complex characters and intricate plots that mesh into multifaceted books, often melding romance, mystery, adventure, history, and the reality of today's society.

Along with advocacy for the homeless, her foreign travels--often to provide medical care in the most remote regions of the world--and her belief in relationship as foundational, underscore her writing process. That, and a lot of Kenyan tea.

When not deep into a project, Laurel hangs out with family and friends, reads, volunteers, and hikes with her

Cavachon puppy, Lucy. And she just happens to be the biggest fan ever of chocolate milkshakes. And hugs.

Facebook: @laurelhouck
Instagram: laurelscottage
Website: laurel-houck-author.com

Merriment, Memories, and Matrimony

A Pinegrove FD Short

By Libby Kay

MERRIMENT, MEMORIES, AND MATRIMONY

Holidays were made for scenes like this, Daisy Mays mused, pouring three mugs of hot cocoa and padding into the living room. Her children, both grown and yet somehow so young, sat on the floor by the Christmas tree. Lights twinkled, soft carols hummed through the speakers as Trevor and Jessie unpacked more decorations for the tree.

"Let me help," Trevor offered, springing to his feet. He took a mug and handed it to his sister before slurping from his own, a chocolate mustache staining his upper lip.

Jessie giggled, pointing at her face. "Trev, you got a little…"

"Wow," he said, wiping his face clean. "I can't believe you didn't use that as an excuse to roast me."

Smirking over the rim of her mug, she asked, "Maybe I'm just mature?"

"You're something," he muttered, flashing a grin before easing back onto a cushion by the tree.

Daisy collected a few smaller boxes, gathering her resolve to have a surprisingly serious conversation despite their festive surroundings. "I wanted to give you both something," she said, keeping her gaze focused on the boxes.

Sensing their mother's tone, both kids grew quiet, their chocolate treats forgotten. "What's up, Momma?" Jessie asked, craning her neck to see better.

The music changed to a familiar tune, Frank Sinatra giving Daisy a little courage as she gingerly opened the boxes. "Jessie," she said, holding out her gift.

"Ohhh," Jessie exhaled, not knowing what was to come.

"Careful, sugar," Daisy said, cupping the delicate ornament in her hand as she passed it to her daughter. "This one is yours." She pivoted to Trevor, handing another orb to her son. "And this one is yours."

Brother and sister sat cross-legged on the floor, as if nearly thirty years hadn't zipped past in the blink of an eye. Daisy was so proud of her children, the sensation threatened to choke her.

Gus, the family basset hound, sauntered over, sniffing in everyone's laps like they were hiding more Christmas cookies. The dog was too smart for his own good, always knowing who to approach first when snacks were involved. This week, the answer was Jessie.

"Hi Gussy," she cooed, digging in her pocket for a dog treat. "I didn't forget about you."

Trevor nudged his sister in the side, attention still fixed on the glass ball in his hands. "Jessie, can we please pay attention? I think Momma's making a memory here."

Jessie stuck her tongue out, ever the bratty sister. "I'm listening, Momma. Ignore this person."

Daisy arched an eyebrow, struggling to stifle her grin. "Y'all need to pay attention, because this house is about to be invaded." She clapped her hands, which startled Gus back to his doggie bed under the bay window. With the Christmas tree up, he had less space to sprawl, but the hound made due.

Straightening her spine, Jessie gave her full attention. Timing was everything, and their peaceful pre-Christmas bubble was about to burst. "What did you want to talk about?"

Gesturing to the ornaments, she smiled sadly. "Now, this is something I meant to do with y'all ages ago. But when your daddy passed, I couldn't bring myself to have this conversation," she breathed, voice cracking on the last word. Trevor and Jessie both scooted closer, but still gave Daisy space to breathe.

Trevor, ever the peace maker, cleared his throat. "Momma, we can save this talk for another time."

"No, we can't." Daisy exhaled, smoothing a hand down her blouse. "The rehearsal dinner is in an hour, and this needs to be discussed." She pointed to the ornaments each of them held, her eyes focused on the task.

"Nick and I bought these ornaments ages ago." She patted her chest, as if willing her heart to stay inside her ribcage. Thinking of her late husband hurt less and less the more time passed, but it didn't mean she still didn't miss him fiercely. At first, losing him had felt tantamount to losing her soul, and while there would always be a gap in her life where he used to be, she'd learned to actually *live* again.

Jessie cocked her head, studying the pink orb cradled in front of her. It was the color of bubble gum, with swirls of flowers dotting the surface. "How come we haven't seen these before?"

Trevor traced a finger through the blue glitter that sparkled in the afternoon light. "Is this a firetruck?" he chuckled, squinting.

"No way!" Jessie gasped, turning hers this way and that until she spied another drawing on the ornament. "Is this is pig?"

A single tear slid down Daisy's face, but she batted it away before her children could notice. "Yes, isn't it incredible?"

"Where did you and Daddy get these?" Trevor's voice dripped with wonder.

Daisy leaned back in her chair, eyes unfocused as she

remembered a fateful trip into town right after they got married. "Your daddy and I were walking down Main Street, after grabbing supper. Kim hadn't yet opened her store, and there used to be a little shop there. Sold knick-knacks and such," she flapped a hand in the air, not losing her flow. "We stopped inside to see about getting Christmas gifts for our parents, and they had a display of blue and pink ornaments." She smiled, happy tears threatening to fall. "Nick went right over to the display, selecting a blue and pink one."

"How old were we?" Trevor asked.

Daisy shook her head. "Y'all weren't even born yet. That's why it was so silly. Your daddy wanted to buy those ornaments, and I kept reminding him we hadn't even had one child, let alone two. But he was determined, said those ornaments spoke to him, and were for our children."

Unable to hold back, Jessie sniffled. "That sounds like Daddy."

"He was so proud of himself, that's for certain," Daisy snickered. "Then the hell of it was, we both forgot about these ornaments for years."

Trevor laughed, low and deep. If they all closed their eyes, it was like Nick was back in the room, his infectious laugh wrapping around them like honey on a warm biscuit. "When did you find them?"

Daisy hummed, drumming her chin. "Only a year before he..." she trailed off. Despite a career with the fire department, their patriarch succumbed to a heart attack on a random weekday. Their most important person gone before anyone could blink. The organ that had cherished his family had let them all down in the end, giving out before anyone was ready to say goodbye.

The room fell silent, save for Gus's snuffles and a hushed sob from Jessie. Once she'd composed herself, Daisy continued. "We were moving boxes in the garage, looking for the Christmas lights, and this little old shoebox fell down and hit your father square in the forehead." Daisy patted her own face and winced. "Left a mark for nearly a week, he got razzed at the station for that, I'll tell ya. When he opened it and saw the ornaments, he screamed like it was a snake. I darted out to investigate, and then we laughed for a solid ten minutes. I joked that we might as well save them for our grandchildren, but he wasn't having it."

Clearing her throat, Daisy lowered her voice in the best imitation of Nick and said, "Honey, we're giving these to Trev and June Bug on Christmas this year. We may have lost some time, but there's still plenty of celebrating ahead of us." This time, Daisy didn't hide her tears. As they fell, she snatched each of their hands. "I wanted to give these to you both now, as a thank you for accepting Paul into our family. Decorate your trees with a little bit of your father, but don't be afraid to make plans for the future."

They were mere hours away from Daisy and Paul's wedding. Who had started as a family friend and colleague of Nick's had morphed into a love and companionship that neither Daisy or Paul expected. Tomorrow, in the firehouse they all loved so much, they'd exchange vows and promise to love and cherish each other. Daisy knew in her heart, Nick would be smiling down on them all.

"We may not have your father here, but we have each other. And what's best, we each have found someone to love and be there for us." Looking to Trevor she said, "Whitney was put on this earth to find you, sugar. Watching you two together, seeing you come back to yourself, has been a joy. I'm so pleased you found her."

Trevor pulled Daisy close, pressing a kiss to her cheek, throat clogged with emotion. "Love you, Momma."

Daisy murmured her own affections before shifting to Jessie. "Sugar, you followed your dreams and saw the world. You helped people and made a difference. But I'm so glad you're home, and especially glad you found your way back to Malcolm. I knew from the moment you met in high school that fate had brought y'all together. Cherish each other, because what you have is special and rare."

"Oh, Momma!" Jessie wailed, collapsing into her mother's arms like she was a little girl.

For a while, the trio huddled close. Gus sensed a shift in the mood and joined the fray. He also managed to snarf down a forgotten marshmallow left in Jessie's mug.

Their sob fest was interrupted when three sets of footsteps walked through the front door. "Yoohoo!" Whitney called out, feet faltering at all the wet eyes blinking back at her. "Lordie! What happened to y'all?"

Paul and Malcolm popped up beside her, matching expressions of confusion on their faces. "JJ? You okay?" Malcolm didn't wait for her answer, closing the distance in three strides and pulling his girl to his chest.

Daisy nodded sadly at Paul who silently joined her, draping an arm around her shoulder to anchor her close. Trevor hopped to his feet, meeting Whitney by the door and kissing her chastely. "Hi darlin'," he pecked the tip of her nose and added, "we're all good. Just having a little moment."

Paul pointed to the open ornament boxes and asked, "I'm guessing you told them?"

"She did," Jessie agreed, dabbing at her face with the hem of Malcolm's shirt. "These are from Daddy," she surmised, voice still trembling with years of grief and love.

Whitney gasped when she saw the ornaments. "Oh, that's magical. How could Nick know how perfect they'd be?"

Jessie held hers out for Malcolm to take. He scoffed, twisting the ornament toward the light. "Is that Oinks?" He was incredulous, grinning at Jessie's moony expression. Oinks was a pig at the farm, Hog Hollow, that Jessie worked at. She loved to tell people that Oinks was her BFF, and Malcolm feared she wasn't kidding.

"As soon as we get home, I'm putting that on our tree," Jessie said.

Malcolm kissed her forehead, breathing in the scent of Christmas cookies and vanilla. "Front and center," he promised.

Inside the kitchen, a timer went off, startling Gus. He barked twice before giving up on his curiosity and falling back into his bed. "Who wants gumbo?" Daisy asked, ushering everyone into the kitchen for supper.

"I can't believe you made your own rehearsal dinner," Whitney tutted, pulling out bottles of sparkling wine from the fridge to toast the happy couple.

Paul chuckled. "I tried to make reservations at the restaurant where we got engaged, but Daisy said she wanted something cozy and casual."

"I think it's perfect," Jessie said, linking an arm through Paul's elbow and resting her head on his shoulder.

"Me too, kiddo," Paul said. "Turns out, your momma knows best."

All six settled into their meals, the mood improved and as festive as it should be before a wedding…and Christmas. The guys joked, the ladies gossiped, and Gus ate more table scraps than he should have, his belly dragging across the floor as he shuffled off.

Daisy reached out, taking Paul's hand and squeezing with all her might. She couldn't take her eyes off Trevor, Jessie and their partners; both couples so in love.

Paul pulled their joined hands to his lips. He kissed her knuckles and winked. Daisy melted in that moment, simultaneously pleased and astounded that fate had given her a second chance at love.

All was right in Pinegrove…

*

After their meal, everyone drove to the firehouse to test the timing of the wedding. Javier and a few other members of Engine 33 were there, greeting them and sharing congratulations. Everyone would be involved in the big day, but it was still special seeing the people that made this town feel like home.

Trevor, Whitney, Malcolm, and Jessie made their excuses when they'd wrapped for the evening. Paul took Daisy's hand, walking her around the back of the station to where he'd parked. He was the chief, and he took advantage of the prime parking spot. "You want me to take the long way home?"

The long way meant driving around Pinegrove, through groves of sturdy pines that gave the town its name. "Yes, please," Daisy agreed, already looking forward to seeing their neighbor's houses decorated and sparkling.

As Paul drove, they listened to more Christmas carols. Wham! and Bing Crosby set the tone for their drive, and Daisy couldn't wipe the smile off her face. They'd all come so far in the last few years, and she couldn't believe their good fortune.

"I wanted to thank you," Paul said when they were stopped at an intersection. He kept staring straight ahead, and Daisy marveled at his profile. He was so handsome, with neatly trimmed gray hair, a strong nose, and a mustache that tickled when they kissed. She felt protected, cherished with Paul. It was not unlike how Nick made her feel, but there was a depth in their relationship, built on decades of friendship and life experiences that just hit different.

"Thank me for what?" Daisy asked, reaching out to lower the volume on Bing. *It was most certainly not going to be a white Christmas in Pinegrove.*

The light changed and Paul carefully pulled back into traffic. His hands were tight on the steering wheel, but his profile was relaxed. "For taking a chance on us, on me. I know Nick left big shoes to fill, but I'm going to do my best to make you happy, Daisy." They'd arrived at Daisy's house, and he cut the engine. Turning to face her he added, "I wasn't looking for anything like this at my age. I figured once I got divorced and hit my fifties, I'd be content with my job and my friends." He cupped her face, smoothing his thumb over her bottom lip. "You're the greatest thing that's ever happened to me, and I love you."

"Oh sugar," Daisy sobbed, hastily unbuckling to pull Paul into her arms for a kiss. Their lips collided, both salty from their tears. "I love you, too. I can't wait to marry you tomorrow."

Paul let out a long, shuddering breath. "Tomorrow can't come soon enough."

For a moment, they sat with their foreheads pressed together, breaths mingling between them. While she savored being close to Paul, neither of their necks could handle this odd angle much longer. "It's a lovely out, why don't we sit on the deck for a moment? I'm not ready to call it a night." Daisy's suggestion brought a smile to Paul's face.

"I'll bring out a glass of wine. Bless her heart, Whitney brought enough over for an army."

A few moments later, they were cuddled up on the swing, legs dangling in the cool air. Daisy rested her head on his shoulder, sipping from her glass. Paul's free hand trailed a path up and down her arms, causing her to shiver.

"I can definitely get used to this," he mused. "Don't get me wrong, it's great when the kids are over, but this," he nestled closer and sighed, "this is perfection. You and me."

"Sugar, you can't get rid of me now," she teased, blinking up at the night sky.

Inside, Gus woofed for some attention, and a fresh bowl of water. "I'll get our boy. You take your time, honey." He kissed her temple, lingering a moment before excusing himself to dog duty.

Despite the cooling temperatures, Daisy wasn't quite ready to go inside. There wasn't a cloud for miles. The sky was inky black, stars sparkling like crystals overhead. Just before she stood, Daisy spied a shooting star streaking across the heavens. She nearly made a wish, but she didn't know what she'd even wish for. She had everything she'd ever need, right here.

Then it hit her, this little sign from the beyond. "Thank you, Nick," she whispered. "We love you." She inhaled, years of memories washing over her. Most folks are lucky to have found love once in their life, but Daisy was truly blessed to have found it twice.

Eyes lingering a moment longer above, she wished a Merry Christmas to Nick, before shaking herself back to the present...and her future.

And with that, Daisy went inside to prepare for her nuptials, to prepare for the next chapter in her life's story. Nick had been right, there was still so much celebrating ahead of them.

After all, this was Pinegrove. Anything was possible...

The End

Don't Miss the Other Books in the Pinegrove FD Series

When Sparks Fly

Two broken hearts, one charming small town, and a few sparks may be the recipe for love...

Whitney Kerr is at a crossroads—literally. After jumping behind the wheel to flee Savannah, and a bad breakup, this Southern Belle is in search of a fresh start. Stopping in a charming smalltown seems like the perfect place to catch her breath and find herself. It's too bad a certain fireman with a crooked grin and kind eyes could have her plans of self-discovery going up in a puff of smoke.

Trevor Mays is at a crossroads—figuratively. Still grieving the loss of his father, he was unceremoniously dumped by his fiancée, who quickly rebounded with his work rival. Just as he thinks things can't get worse, he loses the captain's promotion—to the man who stole his ex. He's about to give up on ever smiling again when a curly-haired beauty with curves for days stumbles into his hometown.

With some help from the residents of Pinegrove, this pair will discover that much like the perfect fireworks show, love only needs a spark.

Fans of Sherryl Woods' <u>Sweet Magnolias</u> series and Sarah Adams's <u>When in Rome</u> series will fall in love with Libby Kay's sweet fireman romance. Ms. Kay's engaging, cozy stories fill your heart and head with possibilities and will quickly become your new favorite!

EXCERPT-

"Thanks for dinner and the walk and the talk." Whitney seemed flustered, and she couldn't keep her mouth shut. "I know it was a rough day, but hopefully it ended on a high note."

Trevor closed the distance in two strides. Reaching up, he tucked a curl behind her ear. His finger grazed her ear lobe as he pulled back, and she shivered. Every cell in his body was on alert at Whitney's proximity. "Tonight was perfect. I can hardly remember why my day sucked."

The admission came easily, and he was incredibly grateful at his mother's matchmaking skills. "I'm glad." Whitney breathed, goosebumps erupting down her neck.

"Good night, darlin'. I'll see you soon."

"See you," she agreed.

Trevor strode to his car and got behind the wheel with a lightness in his step. When the day had started, he'd been certain it would end in disaster. Yet now, with Whitney in town, things just felt better … more hopeful. He hadn't realized until he parked his car that he'd been singing along to the radio the whole drive home. Yeah, Trevor was going to be all right.

Old Flames

Best-selling author Libby Kay romances hearts with her sweet stories about family, friends, and love. Fans of Sherryl Woods' Sweet Magnolias series are finding all the feels with Old Flames, the latest amazing story set in small town America. Don't miss this enduring sweet romance!

Two high school sweet hearts, one charming small town, and flames of chemistry that are hard to deny...

Jessie "JJ" Mays has seen it all. Her job in the Peace Corps has put the world at her feet, with adventure calling with every new assignment. Yet after a decade of traveling, she's become a little lonely—and unable to get over her first love. Soon an emergency phone call from home has her on the next plane, but will her heart survive this visit?

Malcolm "Smithy" Smith loves his smalltown life. His career as a fireman and EMT is fulfilling, his soap opera starlet mother keeps him on his toes, and he's got a great group of friends. The only thing he doesn't have—the love of his life by his side. No matter the distractions, he still misses JJ with a fierceness that consumes him.

When a call to a warehouse fire goes from routine to catastrophic, Malcolm is injured and unable to perform the job he loves. The only upside of having a building fall on him? His girl is back in Pinegrove ready to nurse him back to health. And hopefully, this visit is for good...

With some help from the residents of Pinegrove, JJ and Smithy will discover that sometimes, first love burns brightest.

EXCERPT-

His job. It was the biggest joy of his life. Of course, there was something else that brought him joy, and he'd give anything to see Jessie one more time. If this was the end, that would be the bigger tragedy, not being able to say goodbye. Not being able to hear her laugh, to feel her in his arms ...

The very last thing Malcolm thought about as he closed his eyes was his girl, her warm smile welcoming him to rest. As the smoke wafted around him, he reached out with his free hand, eager to get a touch of her smooth skin. He only hoped she knew how much he missed her, how much he still loved her.

As another chunk of ceiling fell at his feet, faint voices approached Malcolm's prone form. "He's over here," yelled Javi, urgency coating his hoarse cries. "Smithy's over here!"

"Are you sure? I don't see his reflective gear!" Trevor called out, stomping around a pile of debris.

Malcolm closed his eyes and smiled, reassured that his friends were here at the end. He also took comfort knowing that Trevor would take care of Jessie; she was his little sister after all. She would be okay, he mused as he passed out from the pain.

She had to be.

Thanksgiving Overruled

Everyone wants to hear those three little words during the holidays...

Where's the casserole?!

Winnie Kerr wants to utter another three-word phrase to her girlfriend, but Thanksgiving has other plans. After spending far too much time on work, this legal eagle decides an impromptu road trip to visit her sister is the perfect time to tell her girlfriend she loves her. What could go wrong during a few days away from work, right?

Mari Balogh has a problem, she's madly in love with her girlfriend and cannot get those three little words off her tongue. After being burned before from her unsupportive family and a string of bad breakups, this paralegal is guarded. She happily agrees on a road trip to Pinegrove, eager for the space to profess her affections. How hard can it be, right?

From a little trespassing and a kitchen nightmare to a surly cat and a series of misunderstandings, the road to *I love you* is rife with hiccups. Can these two find their way to happily ever after? Or will their relationship go up in a puff of sweet potato casserole scented smoke?

But Pinegrove has proven that love is never overruled!

EXCERPT-

Now Whitney's annoyance nearly radiated through the line. "Win, I'm serious! You, and Mari, deserve a breather." She wasn't certain, but Winnie thought she heard Whitney's foot stomp all the way across Georgia.

Pursing her lips, Winnie pushed off her seat and stalked around her desk. She cupped the back of her neck, willing her traitorous heart to slow. "Mari's fine with bypassing the holiday. We agreed we'll order takeout and just lay low for a couple days."

A loud snort echoed through the phone. "Ha! Give me a freaking break, Win. Granted I don't know Mari well—yet—but I'd wager y'all will be working within five minutes of eating your Kung Pao Chicken."

Winnie opened her mouth to argue, to tell Whitney that her and Mari could enjoy a few days without being glued to their laptops, phone ringers set so they wouldn't miss a single notification. But the words wouldn't come; she'd never lie to her sister.

She imagined it clearly, her apartment cluttered with files, empty takeout containers, open laptops, and a very surly Xena strutting around waiting for extra kibble. Her cat could always tell when it was a special occasion, and she'd set up shop next to her food bowl with a smirk on her face. If cats could smirk, that is…

Whitney gave up waiting for a response and said, "Come to Pinegrove. Daisy is making a whole feast, and we certainly have room for two more."

Return to small-town Pinegrove, Georgia, the romantic setting of Libby Kay's endearing novels, When Sparks Fly and Old Flames, as well as the 2026 novel about another of the hunky firemen in town. Don't miss any of the action or romance!

And Coming in 2026-
Javier's Pinegrove FD Romance

ABOUT THE AUTHOR

Libby Kay lives in the city in the heart of the Midwest with her husband. When she's not writing, Libby loves reading romance novels of any kind. Stories of people falling in love nourish her soul. Contemporary or Regency, sweet or hot, as long as there is a happily ever after—she's in love!

When not surrounded by books, Libby can be found baking in her kitchen, binging true crime shows, or on the road with her husband, traveling as far as their bank account will allow.

Libby cohosts the Romance Roundup podcast with Liz Donatelli where they recommend romance books and interview authors, influencers, and publishers. Check it out for your weekly dose of romance!

Website: https://www.libbykayauthor.com/

Instagram and Facebook: @LibbyKayAuthor
Goodreads and Bookbub: @LibbyKayAuthor

Bl@ze

A The Lost Library Origin Short

By Melissa Koslin

BL@ZE

He stood at McKayla's grave, nothing but a little plaque in the ground in a sea of plaques. The wind blew and ruffled his jacket. The wind was harsh here with no trees to take the brunt. Just cold hard earth dotted with cold hard plaques.

The music he barely heard from a passing car—"O Holy Night," McKayla's favorite Christmas song—should have given him comfort, but it only reminded him that she would miss this Christmas. And every future Christmas.

He never thought they'd kill her. He would have never left her alone.

But he should've known.

McKayla was gone, and it was his fault. He'd known better than to get involved with the Dead King Crew. They'd said they were different, more like a neighborhood organization than a gang. He'd been drunk on the money, alcohol, and the respect from the neighborhood. But he'd grown up over the last year and learned that respect and fear were two different things. McKayla had inspired him to mature and be a real man, not a stupid punk kid.

He kept telling himself she was with God now, the God she loved so much, but it didn't stop the anger.

And he made a decision while standing there.

He was going after him.

He made preparations, and a few days later, he showed up at Sterling Fairfax's mansion on 5th Avenue in New York with his arson tools. He'd done this a hundred times to businesses who wouldn't pay up. He was known as Blaze in the old neighborhood. Everyone knew who had set the fires. Once this was over, he'd never go back there—he wouldn't have Dead King Crew protection anymore.

This time, he'd use those skills for good.

Now to find a way inside. He looked around the garage in the back alley, which had once been a carriage house, past the manicured back garden filled with accent lighting to the imposing four-story limestone building. His extremely dark skin had always been helpful in these endeavors. He didn't have to wear a ski mask to hide in the darkness. He could wear dark-wash jeans and a dark jacket—normal clothes— which helped him look less out of place if someone should happen to notice him.

He mentally diagramed all the cameras he'd spotted to try to find a blind spot. The security was a lot different than he was used to dealing with, but he was sure he could manage.

It was a cool night, so he looked for open windows. There—second story. A tree was fairly close to the corner of the building, and then there was a ledge he was pretty sure was big enough for him to use to shimmy over to the window.

He walked around the outside of the fence to the side where the tree was, which also appeared to block the closest camera fairly well. The camera had probably been installed several years ago before the tree had grown this large. He climbed the fence, and while standing on the top cross post, he just managed to reach a limb of the tree. He scaled the branch hand-over-hand until he was closer to the trunk.

Then he was able to get his feet onto another one. He basically had to climb through the tree to get close to the building, which meant ducking and twisting. He wiped his hands on his jeans to get most of the dirt off and ensure his hands weren't slippery.

The ledge looked just big enough for him to get a decent grip with his fingertips. Before leaving the cover of the tree, he carefully looked around. The night was quiet, perhaps unnervingly quiet for New York City, but then he was in a very different neighborhood than he was used to.

He jumped from the tree and caught the ledge as his body smacked against the stone wall. He had to move quickly—if anyone looked now, they would never miss his dark figure against the white limestone. He shimmied over to the window, stopped just beneath, and paused to make sure the room was quiet and hopefully empty.

Nothing.

He managed to reach up and grasp the windowsill, and then he strained to pull himself up. When he got an elbow over the sill, he paused to look into the room. Looked like a bedroom but was the size of the apartment where he'd grown up. He continued , then got a knee over the sill, and climbed into the room.

There was a fireplace in the room, which he could use to make the fire look accidental, but he wanted it to look like it was caused by negligence, which meant the insurance may not pay out. He didn't want Fairfax simply to be able to build a new mansion for himself, even nicer than this one.

He walked across the room to the door. But that ended up being the closet, or probably more accurately, a dressing room. He tried another door and found the hallway. There was nothing in view either direction, so he slipped out and headed down to the left.

Just before turning a corner, he stopped at the sound of clinking.

He turned to go back the other way, but the next door was too far to reach before whomever was coming down the hall turned the corner.

Then another sound had him glancing around again. Yelling—sounded like from outside.

The clinking sound paused and then rushed away in the other direction.

He risked peeking around the corner. A woman with a graying bun and a black dress—housekeeper?—was rushing away with a tray with a decanter and glass on it. He could see there was only a single glass on the tray, which told him there were probably no guests in the house, just Fairfax.

The housekeeper headed down the stairs. He could see the top of the stair rail—looked like more carved white limestone wrapped in evergreen garland, surely the main staircase.

From this position at the corner, he could hear the yelling voice better. Something about being a father to someone's baby?

"Let the fool inside before he embarrasses Mr. Fairfax in front of the neighbors." He assumed that was the housekeeper giving orders.

"Yes, ma'am." Hurried footsteps, presumably from the entryway, which was surely near the bottom of the stairs. The sound of a door opening and closing, more footsteps.

"What on earth are you yelling about?" the housekeeper asked in a harsh but muted tone, as if trying not to let Fairfax hear.

"That's my baby Fairfax's daughter is having! I'll not be kept away from my child!"

"Mr. Fairfax's daughter is living in France."

"You can get pregnant in France just as easily here."

This was the perfect distraction. He turned and started searching for the best place to set up. He found what looked like a guest bedroom, set a candle close to the curtains, which did not look flame-retardant, and set up his timer. It was a simple device that he'd devised himself, made of components that would mostly burn up, leaving no indication it was arson. He set an alarm on his phone that matched the timer.

Now to find Fairfax.

He hadn't been sure if he'd confront Fairfax, but with that distraction downstairs keeping the staff busy, now was an opportune time.

He tried a few rooms before he came to an office and a man sitting at a desk. On the other side of the room was a fireplace and a huge glittering Christmas tree. For some reason, that tree annoyed him. Maybe because he knew Fairfax didn't actually believe in God, let alone Jesus. He used that tree and all the garland and lights for marketing himself as a good wholesome family man.

Fairfax was faced away from the door, reading something. "What is all that racket?" Surely, he'd heard the door open and assumed it was his housekeeper. When there was no answer, he turned and then stood. "Who are you?!"

"McKayla Garson's fiancé."

"And I should know who that is?"

"You had her killed. I would assume you might know her name."

"A lot of people die. Most of no significance."

Rage surged through his chest. "Why are you sponsoring the Dead King Crew? Rich man like you—why do you care what happens to a bunch of kids in the hood?"

Fairfax smiled as he casually walked across the room. "That's the whole point. I admit Margaret Sanger's scheme is more elegant, but mine works pretty well. Let the cockroaches exterminate themselves." He moved something off the fireplace mantle and pressed a hidden button. Silent alarm?

Blaze glanced back and locked the door then turned back to Fairfax. "Call it off. Tell them you hit it on accident."

"Why would I do that?" Fairfax pressed a panel in the wall and took a gun out of a hidden compartment.

Just as the timer on his phone beeped, Blaze made the decision not to care and moved slowly toward Fairfax. He could try to run, but he barely had a grasp on the layout of this place and the fire had now started. He'd have a hard time getting out and not being caught.

Fairfax aimed his gun at him. "I'll kill you just like I had that stupid girl of yours killed."

"Why? She was a good person. Why did you kill her?"

"You refused to fall in line. She was getting ridiculous ideas in your head about higher powers and purpose. I wasn't about to lose your skillset."

"You killed her because I refused to renounce God?" It had been a new directive sent down. Everyone in the Dead King Crew had to renounce God as part of their membership requirements. He'd read about dictators banning religion, so it didn't set right, and McKayla had been sharing with him her beliefs and experiences with God. He wasn't sure if he actually believed what she did, but he trusted her goodness. He hadn't been able to renounce something that was the center of her life. He'd decided to leave the Dead King Crew.

"You refused not to believe in fairytales. She was the source of it. She had to go."

Blaze clenched his fist. He had other skills, and he would show Fairfax.

Before he took two steps, the door flung open. A young very skinny man walked in—couldn't be older than eighteen, and though he wasn't short, he couldn't weigh more than 120 pounds dripping wet. "You started the party without me? I'm hurt!" He addressed Blaze. "Hang a sec. I'll head out with you."

Blaze just stared. Who in the world was this? He wasn't dressed like one of Fairfax's neighbors, just jeans and a cheap sweater. Then he noticed…was that makeup on the skinny man? A false nose, altered skin tone, and maybe false goatee?

"So…" the skinny man said to Fairfax. "I just popped in to let you know I've found all your fraud and have sent it to the authorities."

"Fraud? What are you talking about?"

"The Carver deal."

Fairfax's arrogant smirk melted.

The skinny man smiled. "Yep. Got all the details on that one. Plus, what were the others? Oh, Spinner, that museum thing, and that dealio up in the Hamptons. Got it all."

Fairfax turned white. Then he aimed his gun at the skinny man and rushed forward.

Blaze stepped in the way and clotheslined him. Fairfax hit the ground with a thud. His breath expelled, and his gun skidded across the floor and under the Christmas tree.

"Ha! Nice!" the skinny man said. "Thanks. As you've probably guessed, my talents reside in the land of cyber, not so much in the land of wrestling. Now, uh, we had better make our graceful and timely exit." He turned for the door, and Blaze followed.

But then he stopped.

The skinny man looked back. "What?"

Then a voice… "Be who she knew you were." The voice was faint, barely a whisper. And he knew without looking around that it had not come from any person.

He felt a moment of calm, like a warm blanket in winter. It reminded him of McKayla's face when she looked at twinkling Christmas lights or watched children playing in the snow—how she knew what was right and good and could find peace in that.

And he knew McKayla had been right about everything.

He went back into the room, picked up Fairfax across his shoulders, and carried him to the door. "The fire is already started, out of control by now. I can't leave him to die."

"We gotta do what we gotta do." The skinny man turned and headed down the hall and then down the stairs. "Take Fairfax out. I'll get the housekeeper and maid." He pulled a chair away from a closet door and opened it as Blaze headed outside.

Blaze set Fairfax on the ground without hurting him.

With the warm glow of white lights adorning the mansion lighting Fairfax's face, Blaze could almost believe there was still some good in the man. He hoped there was. The skinny man came out followed by two women, who looked shaken and confused. "Sorry about that, ladies." The skinny man pressed his hand to his chest and bowed at them. "No hard feelings, I hope."

Then the stranger turned toward Blaze. "Let's book!" He ran between the houses and then down the alley along the back.

Just when Blaze was about to suggest finding someplace to hide, the skinny man grabbed his arm and pulled him into a door of a random building.

Inside was a computer and several monitors set up on a folding table, all with colored lights draped messily across the top. And Trans-Siberian Orchestra's "Christmas Eve In Sarajevo" was playing, which was basically a rock version of "Carol of the Bells" and seemed fitting for this man. On three of the computers looked like surveillance camera feeds—the Fairfax mansion cameras.

"Don't worry, my fine friend," the skinny man said as he took his seat and made a flourish with his hands, "I'll have that camera footage of you deleted in two shakes."

"Who…in the world are you?"

The skinny man spun in his chair to face him and held his hands out wide. "Floyd at your service."

"Okay, Floyd. What in the world were you doing there?"

"Saving your behind, of course."

"I'm confused."

Floyd grinned. "I have that effect." He stood. "Let me start at the beginning. I have been monitoring Fairfax for some time, and imagine my surprise when on the security feed up pops someone breaking into the house? And then I recognized you from the Dead King Crew—I know about that project of his too—and I knew why you were there. How could I let you get caught? So, I flew in for the rescue. Not my usual type of appearance, I'll have you know."

"So, you're like a hacker?"

Floyd kept on grinning. "Pretty quick. I'm impressed."

"And you're totally anonymous?"

"Yep."

Blaze was intrigued. Anonymous but making a difference. Could he do something like that?

And then Floyd grew serious. There's another reason I came. I found something. Something just for you. I need to show it to you before you leave."

"What?" Blaze was still trying to mentally catch up with everything that had happened. This man was like a rabbit on energy drinks. Blaze couldn't keep up.

"Come here." Floyd sat and started typing.

Blaze glanced back at the door but then tentatively moved closer to Floyd.

And up came a picture on the monitor closest to Blaze.

Blaze turned away.

It was a crime scene photo from McKayla's murder. Blood everywhere.

"Forgive me for showing you that." Floyd zoomed in on the image to something right next to McKayla's hand on the floor.

Blaze glanced at the door again but then looked at the screen. "What am I supposed to see?"

"This." He pointed to a spot on the screen. "It was carpet, so it was hard for her to make it clearer. But it's there."

"Is that a…cross?"

"She drew it in the carpet as she was dying."

God was so important to her that she used the last of her strength to stand for him, to honor him.

And he realized…he did believe in God. He'd just been too scared to admit it, scared of the expectations if he became a believer. He could never be as good as McKayla. But he already knew God had expectations for him.

The voice echoed in his head, "Be who she knew you were."

And in that moment, he had a new purpose in life. Be who McKayla—and God—knew he was. He wanted to uncover corruption and help those in need. But with his past, he didn't think he had a lot of options.

He turned to Floyd. "Will you teach me how to be a hacker?"

"Christmas Eve In Sarajevo" ended, and the next song started... "O Holy Night."

Don't Miss the Rest of the Story in

The Lost Library

Her past has caught up with her. Again.

Cali Lebeau has been aiding hackers with her cryptology skills to track an apparent terrorist organization. When they discover what she's been doing, they target her. Asher Cross, billionaire recluse, insists on aiding her, though she doesn't understand why.

Asher Cross has secrets. He must help Cali, keep her alive, but he cannot let her understand his past or his motivations—in order to protect her.

They discover that the terrorist organization is searching for the Golden Library of Moscow, which was first assembled by Ivan the Great and had grown over time to include the oldest and most valuable texts in the world, including missing masterpieces. They believe the library holds black magic and the secret to everlasting life. It was stolen from them by Cali's ancestor, and Cali holds a clue to its location handed down by her mother. In order to free herself and Asher, Cali must race against the terrorists, find the library, and share it with the world.

Will they be able to solve the mystery surrounding

the Lost Library or risk losing their lives?

"You guys! The Lost Library was such a fun book to read! There are layers upon layers of secrets, and author Melissa Koslin does a fabulous job of revealing them one at a time until we MUST know how it all turns out. It's got marvelous vibes of Beauty & the Beast and films like The Librarian, Indiana Jones, Sneakers and National Treasure, so if you are a fan of any of those stories you're going to love this book too!" ~MeezCarrie, Amazon reviewer of *The Lost Library*

Excerpt

Over the next several days, she caught glimpses of him but always from a distance. And he never responded to her request to speak with him.

As she sat at her desk Friday afternoon, she added up how many times she'd seen him around the building recently and realized the frequency had increased significantly from before. And she didn't think she was just being more alert and noticing him more easily. She tended to notice the people around her as a general rule, and the owner of the whole company tended to be more noticeable and memorable than the average cubicle rider.

Finally, she lost patience and went to see the Gray Hats. They were a little surprised at her request but got her the information she requested.

On Saturday morning, she borrowed Floyd's car and headed outside the city to the address they'd found for her.

She pulled off on the side of a rural highway. Could this be right? There was a drive where her GPS said there would be, but it was just a narrow gravel drive buried in trees. She hadn't been exactly sure what to expect—maybe a gated community or some fancy country house—but certainly not a drive with weeds sprouting through it that looked like it hadn't seen a car in ten years.

But the Gray Hats had never been wrong or led her

astray. It took a lot to gain her trust—it was an almost-impossible task—but once a person had it, the trust didn't easily waver.

She turned down the gravel drive.

The lane was narrow and twisted and turned like a serpent. Trees hung low and even brushed the car a few times.

Several minutes passed as she drove deeper and deeper into the woods.

Just as she was about to give up and put the car in reverse, hoping she could navigate back out in reverse, the trees parted. A large house sat in the middle of a clearing barely large enough for the house and circular drive in front of it.

There was no actual yard to speak of. The area in the middle of the circular drive was filled with wildflowers. Trees and various types of vegetation came right up to the house and partially obscured how massive it was. It didn't feel unkempt so much as wild, like the house belonged to the forest.

AVAILABLE IN EBOOK AND PRINT
WHERE BOOKS ARE SOLD.

ABOUT THE AUTHOR

Melissa Koslin is a fourth-degree black belt in and certified instructor of Songahm Taekwondo. In her day job as a commercial property manager, she secretly notes personal quirks and funny situations, ready to tweak them into colorful additions for her books. She and Corey, her husband of twenty-five years, and their young daughter live in Yulee, Florida, where they do their best not to melt in the sun. Find more information on her books at MelissaKoslin.com.

Genesis Day

By Mark Love

DEDICATION

For Kim, Cameron, Travis, Kayo, Ichika and
Yutaka. The stars in my sky.

GENESIS DAY

"Do you have any idea how insane this is?" Gracie said, looking around the room in confusion.

Patrick handed her a glass of wine. "You said life was boring. That you were ready for a change."

"I was thinking of a new hairstyle. Or maybe shaking up my wardrobe. Not a *monumental, life altering* experience." Gracie tried not to gawk at him. There'd been so many things to wrap her head around. Especially the handsome man sitting across from her.

"If somebody told me three months ago that I would be in a new, committed relationship and about to become a guardian for two kids, I'd wonder what type of hallucinogenic they were on."

Gracie stepped out of her shoes. Still holding the wine, she bent and placed them together against the wall. It was an old habit. A comforting one. Barefoot, she walked to the living area and sank into the plush sofa. She savored the wine, letting it slowly glide down her throat. Patrick approached. He carried his own glass, along with a charcuterie board. There were squares of different cheeses, olives, dates, veggies and bunches of grapes. Patrick centered it on the table and sat beside her.

He touched a button on the controller. Soft jazz music played from the stereo speakers. Another touch ignited the fireplace. Automatically, the lights in the room dimmed.

"Are we crazy?" Gracie asked, still watching him.

"Define crazy." He pulled the clips from her dark hair and let it fall to her shoulders. Patrick shifted, drawing her to him.

Gracie closed her eyes, lost in the feeling of his fingers sliding through her hair. Two months together and this guy's touch automatically sent sparks flying through her body, her mind, and her soul. She looked at his face. He was studying her as if memorizing her every feature. He moved slowly, leaning in to kiss her. Gracie's body responded.

She recalled a comment from an old girlfriend. "If your lover is any good, one kiss leads to another. And another. Don't try to count them. Just go with it."

Gracie followed that wonderful advice.

**

She had no idea how much time had passed. The living area was even darker now. The fireplace still glowed. Gracie shifted on top of him. Patrick's arms held her close as they sprawled on the sofa.

"Well, there is no faking my body's reaction to yours," she murmured lazily.

"Right back at you. But I have a confession to make."

"If you tell me that you were a virgin before we met, or that you escaped from some monastery, I'll never believe another word you say!"

Patrick grinned and pulled her up for another kiss. "Wrong on both counts. I was going to confess that I nearly did a celebratory dance when we were paired. Of course, I played it cool. I didn't want to scare you off."

"Smart move, old man." She kissed him back.

"Are you saying that with respect?" he teased.

"Of course. I was always taught it's important to respect my elders. That includes someone such as yourself, who is *so* much older than me!"

"At this point in our lives, a few years isn't much of a difference."

Gracie braced a forearm across his chest, making it easier to look him in the eye. "A few! Twenty-five years is not a few!"

"It is in the grand scheme of things."

"Compared to me, you're a dinosaur." Gracie leaned up and kissed him again. "A very fit, very... *capable* dinosaur. But still a dinosaur."

"Age is just a number. The fact that you're forty should not be held against you."

She opted to ignore his comment. "It still surprises me to think out of all the potential candidates for the colony project, they paired us."

"Can't dispute the science," Patrick joked.

Success at the colony was vital. After generations of devastating wars, global warming, and the erosion of the old earth's atmosphere, relocation to multiple galactic stations was the only solution for the survival of mankind. Decades of research and effort had gone into making the remote facility functional. The infrastructure was in place. Agriculture systems, environment, housing, wind and solar power were all tested under a variety of extreme conditions. The colony was ready to be populated.

Candidates were diligently screened. It was essential that anyone accepted into the program had at least two specialties. Habitation in the colony was somewhat limited. Patrick was an educator, with broad knowledge in multiple subjects. Cooking was one of his passions. His culinary talents included award winning recipes. Having trained with a chemist, he could combine ingredients and spices to make any basic meal extraordinary.

Gracie was a physician. Her practice ran the spectrum from pediatrics to geriatrics and everything in between.

Gracie was part of an international family that traveled extensively. She had a gift for languages and was fluent in five.

Of over three million potential candidates, The Copernicus System matched them. Cognitive testing, physical fitness, personality profiles, goals, dreams, lifestyle beliefs, and more were analyzed. The Copernicus System's foundations were reminiscent of the dating applications that were extremely popular back in the early twenty-first century. But Copernicus enhanced those algorithms a thousand percent to ensure accuracy.

Gracie and Patrick were allowed twenty-four hours alone to make the final determination regarding their compatibility. As Patrick said, there was no disputing science. He was intrigued by her intelligence and her beauty. She was curious. Within six hours they became lovers. By the eighth hour, they were ready to make the commitment.

"When do the kids arrive?" Gracie asked.

"Tomorrow morning at first light. Gives us a week to get acclimated." Patrick was running his fingers through her hair again.

"We should get some sleep. This may be the last time we get to fool around on the sofa."

"As long as we're under the blanket, it shouldn't be a problem," Patrick said.

She gave him a wicked smile. "These kids will be impressionable. We don't want to scar them by witnessing your wanton acts of sexual prowess."

"Seems to me, you started the action this evening."

"Complaining?"

"Never," Patrick said.

Gracie rolled off the sofa and made her way to the bedroom. He deactivated the fire and music and carried the empty wine glasses and charcuterie board into the kitchen. First light would be here soon.

**

Patrick and Gracie were among half a dozen couples waiting at the arrival portal. There was a rumble of nervous chatter. Everyone was anxious. Patrick nodded in acknowledgement at two women across the room, clutching hands. He recognized Joan, the short blonde, from department meetings at the school. Rachel was her partner. Her background was in one of the engineering fields.

Each couple would be welcoming their new family members. The others would be receiving one child, whose age would be anywhere from six to sixteen. All the kids were orphans. Patrick and Gracie were awarded two siblings, a brother and sister. As with the adults, they had undergone similar screening to be accepted in the colony program. Since she was on the medical team, Gracie was privy of the medical files for all the children.

"We got first dibs," she said softly.

Patrick squeezed her hand. "Did you snoop?"

"Only a little. For some reason, we were already slated to be matched with them. The Copernicus System must have found similarities between us and their biological parents. Maybe their father was part dinosaur."

"Keep that up. I'll tell the kids to call you Momasaurus."

A chime sounded. The arrival portal slid open. A member of the flight crew began escorting the children out. As each one cleared the portal, a pair of adults stepped forward. Handshakes and hugs followed. Gracie shifted her weight from one foot to the other. Patrick recognized this as a sign of impatience. He smiled. Two months together and he could already read her body language.

"There!" Gracie released his hand and rushed across the chamber.

Sean and Bella wore nervous smiles. Both kids were lean, with dark hair and eyes. Sean was twelve. He was already taller than Gracie. Bella was nine. She was petite. Bella ran toward her, wrapping her arms around Gracie's waist. This was their first meeting in person. Numerous video coms during the last month helped begin forming a connection. It was a great way to learn about each other.

Sean remained in place, watching his sister and Gracie embrace. Both females seemed to be talking simultaneously. Patrick moved over beside the young man.

"Welcome to the colony." He held out a hand.

Sean hesitated. "My dad and I used to hug, every time we got together. Would you mind if we did that?"

"Not at all." Patrick pulled the boy close. He felt Sean's arms go around his back. The kid squeezed him tightly. They stood that way for a time.

"Trade partners?" Gracie asked from behind him.

"Of course." Patrick released Sean and moved aside as Gracie hugged him. Patrick looked at Bella. She raised her arms. He scooped her up and embraced her.

"You're a lot taller than I expected," Bella said. "Older too!"

"Video coms aren't always reliable."

A flight crew member approached them. He extended his forearm toward Patrick. There was a silver band three inches wide imbedded in the arm.

"Just a formality. Final step in the process," he said.

Patrick had a similar implant. They all did. He held it out to the crewmember. A soft chime sounded. The transfer was complete. Patrick and Gracie were now the official guardians of the kids.

"Let's go home," Gracie said.

**

All the children's belongings had been transported to the living quarters. It was designed in what was referred to on old Earth as a bungalow. There was a master suite on the main floor. Upstairs were two standard bedrooms, separated by a bathroom. Sean and Bella would have their own space. Patrick and Sean moved the containers into the appropriate rooms. Gracie helped Bella unpack and get organized.

The colony's design incorporated many of the components of old Earth. The living quarters were similar to neighborhoods from the era of the 1950s. In addition to bungalows, there were ranch style dwellings and duplexes, which were intermixed with the bungalows. The intent was to develop communities where the residences would form relationships. Socialization was a key ingredient to achieving a satisfactory lifestyle.

There was one dome that protected the colony. Residents could use solar powered trams to travel the region.

Patrick looked at Sean with a raised eyebrow. "Want some help?"

"Rather do it later. Do we have food?"

"C'mon. We'll make lunch."

Sean was skeptical. "Do we have to eat, like space food? Stuff that looks like yogurt but is supposed to have all the nutrients of hamburgers?"

"No. We have real food, just like back on old Earth."

In the kitchen, Patrick showed him the layout. There was a traditional oven and stove. The refrigerator and freezer were well stocked. Boxes of cereal, crackers and loaves of bread filled the pantry.

"Want a burger?" Patrick asked.

"Yes! Does Dr. Gracie cook?"

Patrick shook his head. "Only occasionally. The kitchen is my territory. You can help put lunch together. Been a long time since I made burgers."

The guys prepared the meal. Patrick showed Sean how to lightly toast the buns and arrange the toppings on a platter so everyone could make their own choices. The aroma of the meat grilling attracted Gracie and Bella.

"Hamburgers! And pickles!" Bella said with glee. "No more space food? It all looks like snot!"

"We'll have regular meals. It may take us a while to learn what kind of things you like," Gracie said. "But Patrick is a chef. He can make just about anything you want."

They gathered around the table and enjoyed the food. Relaxed conversation flowed. Patrick noticed Bella kept nudging her brother. Sean glared at her.

"Something wrong, Bella?" he asked.

She sighed dramatically. "Sean was supposed to ask, but he's trying to be polite and wait for the best time."

"Ask what?"

Bella pushed her empty plate to the side. "What we're supposed to call you? We had real parents..."

"Biological parents," Sean said quietly.

"Yes, biological parents. Our Mom and Dad. But they're gone now. And we're living here, on the colony, with you guys."

"We're your guardians," Gracie said. Gently, she took the girl's hand.

"Right. But it feels funny calling you Dr. Gracie and Patrick. And it doesn't seem right to call you Mom and Dad. Because you're not."

"No one can replace your parents," Gracie lauded. She wasn't their mom but she'd hoped they would grow to love her as one.

"We don't want to upset you. Or make it uncomfortable," Sean cautioned.

Patrick cleared his throat. "Far as I'm concerned, you can call us anything you'd like."

"Whatever you want." Gracie couldn't keep the hope from her voice.

"Can I call you Doc?" Bella asked her.

"Of course."

The young girl threw her arms around Gracie's neck. "Hiya, Doc."

"Hiya, Bella."

Sean was pleased with that. He glanced at Patrick. "Got a nickname?"

"Nope. Something tells me I'm about to get one."

"Can you make desserts too?" Bella asked him.

Patrick nodded. "Do you have something special in mind?"

"Maybe."

He pulled a small container from the counter. "I made these yesterday, to celebrate your arrival." Patrick handed the container to Bella. She popped the lid.

"Cookies!"

"Oatmeal with dried cranberries and orange zest, dipped in dark chocolate."

Bella took two, passed the container to Sean, who also took a pair. Gracie and Patrick watched the kids bite into the treats and the smiles that followed.

"No more space snot!" Bella cried. "Can I call you Cookie?"

"Sure," Patrick said with a smile.

Bella jumped from her chair, ran around to where he sat and hugged his neck. "Hiya, Cookie."

"Hiya, Bella."

"Glad we got that settled," Gracie said. The joy in her heart felt complete.

**

Over the next few days, the children settled into a routine. After breakfast, there was time for exploration, learning firsthand about the colony and how everything worked. The four of them would wander various quadrants. Sean showed an interest in making the meals. Patrick, now officially dubbed Cookie, explained the processes for creating tasty dishes. Bella watched closely, eager to serve as a taste-tester.

The night before the holiday, they sat around the fire. Gracie accessed historic films from the Copernicus System. There was no need for a monitor or screen. The various characters were visible as holographs. She let the kids choose.

Patrick had been busy after dinner, but he wasn't in the

kitchen area. He joined them halfway through the first viewing, an animated feature. Gracie slid beside him on the sofa. The kids were sprawled on the floor, engrossed in the story.

"What are you up to?" she whispered in his ear.

"A little welcome gift."

"I didn't know old dinosaurs could be mysterious."

"That's how we last so long."

Gracie snuggled against him. Patrick's arm drew her close, his fingers lightly stroking her back. Sparks of excitement jumped beneath her skin. Gracie was still amazed at their connection.

After a while, she noticed both kids yawning. Gracie ended the program. "Time for bed. Tomorrow will be a long day."

They watched the kids trudge up the stairs to their rooms. Gracie started to get up from the sofa, but Patrick pulled her back. Before she could say a word, he kissed her. Softly at first, then with more passion. The excitement intensified, causing her body to shiver. Then she heard Bella shriek.

Patrick drew back. Reluctantly, Gracie pulled away from him. But not before seeing the mischief on his face.

"Come see! Come see!" Bella called.

Upstairs, they found the girl bouncing up and down, just like one of the animated characters from the holograph. She pointed at a frame on the wall. Sean was standing behind her, smiling. Gracie saw an image there of Bella, Sean and their parents. Then it shifted. Another one appeared. It held for a moment or two, then was replaced by yet another.

"It's ancient technology," Patrick said. "Not the same as a memory scan. This is a reel of images, what the older generations called pictures or photographs. This way your parents will always be with you."

"There's one in my room too," Sean said quietly. "Thank you."

"You're welcome."

Gracie stared at him in amazement. "When did you learn how to do this?"

"Dinosaurs understand ancient technology."

**

It was time. There were some similarities to certain ritualistic holidays from various cultures on old Earth. Today was Genesis Day. This would officially mark the new beginning of the colony. The final members of the population were in place. It was a day of celebration. A gathering of all five thousand people. Leadership was established. Tomorrow everyone would assume their various duties and responsibilities.

Tables were laden with food from different regions, different cultures. Bella clung to Doc's hand. She looked in wonder as Gracie engaged others, speaking in several languages without the aid of an interpreter or device.

"How do you know all this?" she asked.

Doc smiled. "I traveled extensively on old Earth. Sometimes I would stay in a region or country for several years, helping people. It was easier when I knew or could learn the language."

Sean and Patrick enjoyed the variety of food. They met other new families. Patrick saw the hesitation from the kids, cautiously meeting others their own age. This is how friendships grow. How relationships would start.

The colony's dome provided protection for space's elements. It was large enough to allow for a simulated fireworks display, dazzling colors of lights and sounds to mark the occasion.

A new beginning. For Patrick, Gracie, Sean and Bella.

For them all.

Genesis Day.

The End.

Don't Miss More Romances by Mark Love

Devious

Jamie Richmond, reporter turned author, is doing research for her next book. Attempting to capture the realism of a police officer's duties while on patrol, she manages to tag along for a shift with a state police trooper. A few traffic stops and a high speed chase later, Jamie's ride takes an unexpected turn when she witnesses the trooper being shot.

Although it is not a fatal injury, Jamie becomes obsessed with unraveling the facts behind this violent act. While she is trying to sort out this puzzle, she becomes romantically involved with Malone, another trooper with a few mysteries of his own. Now Jamie's attention is divided between a blooming romance and solving the crime which is haunting her.

Jamie begins to question the events that took place and exactly who could be behind the shooting. It was a devious mind. But who?

EXCERPT-

Suddenly, I saw a flash of light and heard a muffled bang. Smitty pitched onto his back, his right hand clawing feebly at his holster as a loud roar reached my ears. The door of the truck was still open, a brown arm extended beyond the edge of the spotlight. A gun was clutched in the gloved hand. I watched in horror as the trigger was pulled back for another shot.

Everything that happened next must have been instinct. Or maybe it was merely a reaction. Or dumb luck. Or the Force. Yeah, maybe it was the Force. I don't think I'll ever know for sure.

I reached across and pounded on the horn with one hand, flipping the buttons Smitty had used to activate the siren with the other. The sudden noise startled the driver. His arm jerked back into the cab and the door slammed. Spraying stones and dust behind, the truck lurched onto the road and raced away.

Fumbling the microphone off the dash, I thumbed the button. "Kleinschmidt has been shot! Send an ambulance!" I dropped the microphone and managed to get my door open. The frame around the window clipped my forehead and knocked me back a step.

I'd forgotten to turn off the siren and its wail was splitting my eardrums. "Idiot," I muttered, "stay calm." This was easier to say than it ever was to do.

Reaching back inside, I switched the siren off then rushed around to the front of the car. Smitty was lying on his back on the edge of the road. Blood soaked the gravel beneath him. His eyes were closed, but I could see his chest moving.

I dropped to my knees beside him. "You're going to be okay, Smitty. I called for help."

Vanishing Act

When Jamie's best friend vanishes, she'll do anything to find her and bring her home.

A new year marks new beginnings for Jamie Richmond. Not only has she moved into a cozy new house, but she's brought Malone along with her to fan the flames of their growing romance. When Jamie's best friend, Linda Davis, enters the picture, she thinks everything is right with the world.

Linda begins a May-September romance with Vincent Schulte, Jamie's doctor and good friend. But while Vince is sweeping Linda off her feet, she unknowingly has captured the attention of a stalker. The idyllic life suddenly takes a very bad turn when Linda disappears without a trace on a cold and snowy day. The police are scrambling to find a clue that will lead them to Linda.

Malone does his best to comfort Jamie and encourages her to let the professionals do their job. But if there's one thing he's learned in their time together, it's that nothing will stop this stubborn redhead from solving this mystery.

Jamie turns all of her attention on figuring out who took Linda and where she might be, regardless of the dangers she may face. Her efforts once again put her in harm's way. But will she find her best friend?

EXCERPT-

"So are you going to tell me what's going on, Linda? You've been beaming a thousand-watt smile."

I saw the color radiate on her cheeks. She lowered her eyes and took a sip of her coffee. Finally, she drew a deep breath and raised her face.

"I think I'm in love."

I sat back in amazement.

"Vince came over last night. After dinner, we moved to the sofa. The fire was lit and one light was on low. I had been in a rush when I came home, so I hadn't bothered to change."

"So we're just listening to music. And I mentioned that I had to get out of my boots. My feet were starting to cramp. That's when things got…different."

"What do you mean, different?"

"Vince told me to move to the other end of the sofa. Then he slowly unzipped my boots and pulled them off. My legs were on his lap. He started to massage my feet, chasing away the aches and pains. Then he moved up to my ankles. And the whole time, he just kept talking, keeping his voice very low and soft."

"What did he say?"

Linda shuddered with the memory. "He told me all of the things he was going to do to me, all the ways he wanted to please me. It was like I was hypnotized. He was in total control of me. I couldn't move."

No words found their way out of my mouth.

"I swear he touched on every fantasy, no matter how dark, I have ever considered. And the whole time, he just kept talking softly, massaging my legs. Jamie, by the time he finally undressed me, I was so far over the edge, I didn't think I'd ever make it back."

Fleeing Beauty

A discovery of priceless artwork leads Jamie on a collision course with danger.

Jamie Richmond used to live a nice, quiet life. But last fall she witnessed the shooting of a police officer and figured out who did it. Then this winter saw her best friend targeted by a stalker and kidnapped. Yep, Jamie solved that one and came to the rescue. Now it's summertime and the living is supposed to be easy. All she wants to do is write her novels and spend free time with Malone, the guy who has been by her side since all this craziness began. But that's not likely to happen.

Jamie's father was a very successful sculptor who tragically died more than twenty years ago when she was just a child. What she remembers about him is little more than bits and pieces. A storeroom filled with crates of his work is discovered in an old converted factory. This potential fortune in artwork has been waiting all these years.

Jamie recruits Malone and a few close friends to help her unpack the crates and bring her father's gifts out to the light of day. News of this discovery leads to a robbery. Now Jamie is determined to figure out who is behind the crime.

EXCERPT-

This sculpture was titled "Fleeing Beauty".

It was a woman caught in the act of running. Tendrils of slender marble in various lengths and thicknesses extended from her head, as if they were locks of hair billowing out behind her. Part of her face was obscured, turned against her shoulder as if attempting to hide her features from whoever was chasing her. The woman's body was voluptuous, full of dangerous curves. There was something haunting about this piece. The guys became quiet, which was unusual. Linda slowly moved around it, taking pictures.

"Holy shit," Ian muttered.

"Watch your language," Malone said, cuffing him lightly on the back on the head.

"How did he do that?" Ian said, taking a step away. "She looks real."

"She looks alive," Malone said.

"Check the file," I suggested.

None of us could take our eyes off the sculpture.

We spread the file out on the worktable. There were pictures of a woman standing in front of a drop cloth. She was blonde, with an impish smile on her face. She could have been in her early to middle twenties. It was impossible to tell how tall she was. Her figure was eye catching, with a tiny waist and round hips. Most of the pictures showed her in a one piece bathing suit. There was one where she wore a sheer negligee. There were shots of her standing on a pedestal, others with her arms outstretched, and still others where she was looking over her shoulder. In a couple of photos he must have used a fan to blow her hair back.

"She's a doll," Ian said.

"Jamie, I think this is the most beautiful thing I've ever seen," Linda said softly.

"You'll get no argument from me."

AVAILABLE IN EBOOK AND PRINT WHERE BOOKS ARE SOLD.

ABOUT THE AUTHOR

Mark Love (yes, that's really his name) lived for many years in the metropolitan Detroit area, where crime and corruption are always prevalent. A former freelance reporter, Love is drawn to mysteries and the twists and turns that mirror real life. He is the author of "Why 319?" and three books in the Jamie Richmond Series "Devious" "Vanishing Act" "Fleeing Beauty" "Stealing Haven" and "Chasing Favors" and several short stories.

Love resides in west Michigan with his wife, Kim. He enjoys a wide variety of music, reading and writing fiction, cooking, travel, most sports and the great outdoors. You can find his website at the link below.

https://motownmysteries.com

Adoring Alex

(A Persuading Lucy Origin Short)

By Tammy Mannersly

DEDICATION

To Rita, Ian and Bonamie. Your love and encouragement inspires me to keep trying every day.

ADORING ALEX

Alex had missed the *sexy* memo. The one that instructed most of the girls at Toby Sutton's senior year Halloween party to find a costume that was nothing less than sex kitten. In fact, there were cat costumes, and bunnies. A few short-skirted maids with feather dusters and a police officer complete with the baton and handcuffs.

"Don't you dare smirk at me. I'm not kidding." At the kitchen island, Alex's friend Madison Foley was pointing her finger in accusation at Claire Ivers. Both had dressed as sexy nurses and from what Alex had overheard of the conversation, Madison was threatening another drinking challenge.

Just as Alex was about to make her escape from the commotion, she heard the shout of a familiar voice over the ruckus of pop music and laughter. Callum Hawthorne—popular charmer that he was—had his arm around a new girl as he yelled out to his bestie, Lucy Spencer. Though Lucy was having none of it. With a flick of her wrist, she waved him off. As Cal disentangled himself and chased after Lucy trying to persuade her to come back, Alex noticed that they had both been receivers of the aforementioned memo. And they were matching. *Sexy pirates. What a great costume choice.*

Alex grumbled as she hurried down the corridor and ducked into the bathroom. She locked the door and looked over her reflection in the mirror. Had she received a heads up about the dress code, she might have dressed differently. Instead, she'd chosen to dress as the best friend of a beloved childhood wizard. It had been such an easy costume to put together—black and burgundy robe, white school shirt and tie—and she could let her naturally wild curly hair be free. She'd thought it so perfect and cute until faced with the realisation it wouldn't offer her the kind of attention she'd hoped for tonight.

Knock knock. It was a forceful rap of knuckles against timber. "Are you done? Some of us need a refresh."

Bethany Jonston. The voice—or maybe it was the attitude—was easily recognisable.

Alex groaned. There would be no luck catching Jesse Harding's eye while Bethany was around. She'd called dibs at softball training on Thursday, saying that Jesse was her pick of the boys this senior season. To go against that decree was to risk physical injury or worse—social expulsion.

"Hello?" Bethany knocked again, harder this time. The doorknob rattled with her efforts to get in.

Alex assessed her appearance one final time and sighed. She didn't want to wimp out and go home. Toby's parties were legendary. *Everyone* was here. She had to suck it up and stick it out. Better to be dorky Hermione than Norman Jones from her chemistry class who'd confessed upon her entry to the party that he was *too cool* to wear a costume. *He was not.* Toby's dodgy friend Rouso and the baseball team were quick to point this out and send him packing. No costume, no entry apparently.

"Look, if you don't come out right now, I'll call the cops or the fire department or something," Bethany threatened. "It's got to be illegal to hog the bathroom when others have lipstick to reapply."

Alex yanked open the door to see her teammate dressed

in the tiniest softball player outfit she'd ever seen. It was a bikini except for the addition of knee-high socks and sneakers. And as expected, the perfectly proportioned stunner pulled it off as though it were designed for her.

"Alexandra Morganson. Should have known it was you." Bethany gave Alex a quick once over. "I'm sorry to say, you can't fix ugly, lovely."

Alex thinned her lips as she pondered over the price she'd pay for an angry retort. Bethany wasn't captain of the team, but her bestie Cherish was. Still, she didn't want to be on the outs like Tanya Stoddard. No one had been allowed to throw the ball to her for a week no matter how much Coach Hansen had ordered.

Alex forced a smile as she went to step over the threshold. "It's all yours, Beth—"

A commotion in the corridor drew their attention.

"Someone call for the fire department?" Cherish—dressed in a cheerleader crop-top and pleated skirt—laughed as she dragged Jesse Harding along with her. Jesse's mates trailed behind with jeers and laughter. Seeing their varied states of undress, Alex knew they too had likely been made aware of the sexy dress code.

Jesse was half naked in what was left of his fireman costume. Black boots, yellow pants and red suspenders looked mouth-wateringly gorgeous mixed with that rock-hard chest and rolling abs. And he was wet.

Did someone turn the fire hose on him? Is that why he's now shirtless? Maybe he hadn't had a shirt to begin with? Alex caught herself staring. It was hard to look away from those abs. When she finally did, she caught Jesse staring right back. His little smile had her heart flip-flopping.

Cherish pushed Jesse forward and he stumbled to a stop before colliding with Alex. He was too close now. Alex couldn't hold his gaze. Her pulse raced as she fought her inner she-devil. Jesse's mouth had looked so soft and kissable. She thought of the intensity of his stare. *Had he been thinking the same about me?* Alex curled her hair behind her ears as a warm blush crept over her cheeks.

"Keen for seven minutes in Heaven, Bethany?" Cherish teased as she gestured to the bathroom.

I am. Alex had to bite her tongue and fight not to raise her hand in eagerness as she saw her team captain's suggestive wink. One of the baseball boys behind them barked in encouragement, earning himself a round of laughter from his friends.

"I can guarantee you some much needed privacy," Cherish continued.

"Yeah, nah. I don't think—" Jesse attempted to back up a step, but Cherish playfully shoved him toward the bathroom.

"You're not getting out of it that easily," she told him.

Jesse let out a nervous laugh, but otherwise kept his cool composure. Being the popular jock came with attention and Jesse's endurance of the spotlight had proven he wasn't easily ruffled, but he wasn't *easy* either. Alex had heard the stories, knew Jesse had been on his fair share of first dates, but had never settled on a girlfriend. She'd witnessed his friends teasing him for it, knew girls like Bethany saw winning him over as a challenge. Alex on the other hand was captivated by his kind heart and generous soul. She knew he'd been the anonymous donor to replace her kit when it had been stolen. The softball glove alone would have cost more than she made in a week working casually at the local fish and fries place. It also helped that Jesse was the hottest guy she had ever laid eyes on. Hazel eyes, perfect teeth. The little dimple on his cheek. And that body—*was it getting hot in here?* Alex fanned herself with her hand as she considered just how appropriate Jesse's fireman costume seemed.

She sighed lost in her own little fantasy and immediately regretted drawing attention to herself. At Jesse's soft chuckle, Alex cleared her throat. *Geez, could I be more obvious? How embarrassing.*

"Love the thought, Cherish-honey." Bethany's clipped

tone brought Alex's attention back to the actual matter at hand. "But I'd have to be desperate to try something in this filthy bathroom when there are like three guest bedrooms in this place."

Cherish gasped in approval. "Oh my gosh, of course, babe. I've got a hold of this one. Just lead the way." She tightened her grip on Jesse and took a step forward.

"Hang on." Jesse pleaded, but when Bethany and Cherish ignored him, he planted his feet firmly and tried again. "Wait a minute."

"What's up love?" Bethany twirled her manicured fingers in the air expressively as though she didn't have time for the hold up.

"Not sure I'm feeling this," Jesse told her.

"Dude wants to do *it* in the bathroom," Nate Needham—dressed as a gladiator complete with sword— hooted from where he stood huddled with the pack of baseball teammates.

"Ew, you so dirty, man," Tim Garber—resident Tarzan in his little loin cloth—guffawed as though the mere thought was the funniest thing. His laughter became contagious amongst his friends until everyone was chuckling. A few of the guys took it upon themselves to mimic some racy moves in case anyone required clarification.

Alex gave them a look of concern. This was not the baseball team she was used to. *Did they bathe in alcohol? Maybe that's why Jesse's wet?* She braved a glance at him, caught him side-eyeing his buddies, only minorly infected by their giggle-fit. When his eyes met hers again, he winked. It took Alex's breath away.

Bethany cleared her throat aggressively. "How super cute. It looks like our little Alexandra has a crush on my man."

Alex's soul left her body. *Oh crap.*

"What?" Cherish nearly spat out her chewing gum and shot a glare Alex's way. Alex hadn't even noticed her team captain had been chewing gum in the first place.

"Um—" Alex squeaked. What could she say? She really didn't want to end up like Tanya. She loved softball.

When Cherish clenched her hand into a fist and stepped forward, Bethany held her back. "No, hon. It's okay. We just need to teach this little bitch a lesson." Bethany crowded Alex's personal space and gave her a shark-like smile.

"Oh, dude it's on," one of the guys quipped.

"Chick fight," someone in the back declared hopefully.

Alex felt her skin grow cold and clammy. She gulped. *What fresh hell am I in for?*

"You really think you stand a chance with a snack like Jesse, little lonely Alexandra? Well then, maybe it's time we give you the opportunity you so desperately crave?" Without warning, Bethany shoved Alex back into the bathroom, causing her to stumble over her own feet. "You've got seven minutes, babe," Bethany warned before yanking Jesse's arm from Cherish and forcing him over the threshold beside her. "I'd make them count if I were you. If you haven't made it on the scoreboard before your time is up, then we'll all know what a true loser you really are." Bethany turned a pitying expression on Jesse. "Scream for help if you need it, all-star." She kissed her fingers and touched them to his cheek. "I'll just be right outside if you need me." Then she pulled the door shut on them with a loud *bang*.

It took Alex a second or so to compute what had just happened. She could still hear the *thump-thump* of the music blasting through the speakers in the main living areas and the giggles and laughter of her teammates and the boys right outside the door. But everything was muffled in the smaller, tiled space of the bathroom. Yet her racing heart beat sounded incredibly loud her in ears.

Jesse cleared his throat and Alex nearly jumped out of her skin as the sound reverberated off the walls around them.

"Sorry." Those lovely hazel eyes filled with apology when she met them again.

"No—" Alex shook her head and then raked her fingers through her hair. "Uh—no worries." She wrung her hands to stop them from shaking, didn't know if she could also hide the trembling of her lower lip. This was exactly what she'd dreamed of. Her and Jesse. Alone. Scratch the bathroom location. And now she was going to blow it.

Jesse perched on the edge of the porcelain bathtub, all those abs and muscles bunching and flexing deliciously. "Bethany sure dances to her own tune, right?"

Alex choked back a laugh. "That's probably the mildest way I've heard someone describe it."

"Well, you're friends, aren't you? Teammates at least. I don't want to bad mouth her and have you thinking poorly of me."

What? "How could I ever think poorly of you after what you did for me?" *Oh crap.* Alex covered her mouth with her hand. She hadn't wanted Jesse to find out she knew the truth. He'd made such a point of saving her anonymously.

"After what I did for you?" Jesse narrowed his gaze in curiosity, but his small smile betrayed him. "I'm not sure I know what you mean."

What should I do? Should I tell him? I've already put my foot in it.

"Two minutes down, guys," Cherish yelled through the door.

"Hope you're making this time count, Morganson." Bethany had a knack for making something so simple sound so threatening.

Alex sighed and took a seat beside Jesse. She was proud of herself for not flinching when her thigh rested alongside his. Even that small touch seemed to spark straight through to her skin. Maybe Bethany had been right about this being Alex's opportunity. Thanking Jesse for all he'd done for her would be a win even if he wasn't interested in anything more.

She looked up into those beautiful hazel eyes, wished she could gaze into them forever, studying the flecks of green, brown, and gold. "I have a friend at the sporting goods store," Alex confessed. "She saw you buy the new kit. All the things I'd had stolen from our last game away. Then they were just donated back to me by some generous sponsor." Alex let her gaze fall to the floor as she grinned at the memory, remembering her switch from broken-hearted to elation upon receiving the duffle bag of gear. "I know it was you. I know what you did for me." She swallowed back the lump in her throat. Gosh, his kindness had meant so much to her. "Thank you," she told him and hoped he could feel the depth of her sincerity in those words.

He was silent for a moment and it had her risking a peek at him. Jesse was also staring at the floor, but he was smiling. Alex's heart swelled hopefully. That had to be a good sign.

"I'm sorry." Nerves had her croaking out the words. "I know you didn't want anyone to find out."

He chuckled quietly.

Is that relief? Alex bent her head to try to catch his gaze. She wanted to say sorry again.

"You're pretty extraordinary, do you know that?"

Alex's heart stopped. "Me?" Another squeak. Her cheeks heated with embarrassment.

Jesse finally looked up at her. There was something in his eyes, a look Alex had only ever seen from her parents. *Adoration?* "Yes, you, Alexandra Morganson. The first time I watched you play it took my breath away. The passion. Determination. You try your hardest every time. I've seen you do the same in class, with your friends. You are your best in every aspect of your life. You inspire me to do the same."

Alex couldn't feel her body. *Have I died? Is this heaven?* She stared at Jesse's lips again. So sweet, so gentle, so kissable—just like the guy sitting next to her.

"When some jerk hurt you by taking your gear after that game up north," Jesse winced as though the memory itself was visceral, "I had to do something. I couldn't stand to see you like that. So sad. Deflated. You were like this beacon of hope and joy that suddenly lost its light. I had to fix it. So I did."

"But why you?" The words left Alex's lips before she'd thought them through.

Jesse shifted slightly, facing her. His knee now even firmer against her own. "I had to," he told her again as though there wasn't another option. "But you weren't supposed to find out. I didn't want to ruin things. We're friends—sort of. I wasn't sure if you even noticed me. Not the way I noticed you." He shook his head, started to look worried. "I don't know if this is coming out right. But if you found out that I like you, I—" Jesse bit his lower lip and his eyebrows furrowed.

If you found out that I like you. The words repeated themselves over again in Alex's mind like a mantra. *Jesse likes me. Me? Plain Alex Morganson?*

"Two minutes, loser," Bethany yelled through the bathroom door. "Better try something soon or be the laughing stock of the year."

There was further chatter on the other side of the door and then a burst of laughter, but Alex was much too distracted by what had just unfolded with Jesse to care.

"You like me?" The awe in her words irked her. *Oh my gosh, am I twelve?*

"Look at you," Jesse gestured to her whole person— dorky Hermione outfit, wild curly hair, average human shape and all. "How could I not?"

A firework exploded through all her nerve endings. She felt her heart somersault in her chest. *Is this really happening?* She tried to catch her breath. "I like you, too."

Jesse's whole expression lit up with her words. "I'd been so worried, but the way you looked at me tonight gave me hope. I didn't want to go another Halloween, another party, another day without getting the chance to properly talk to you. To tell you how I feel."

"Sixty seconds. Fifty-nine. Fifty-eight." Bethany began a countdown and was quickly joined by her bestie in ticking off the numbers.

"I guess I should probably thank Bethany for giving me the opportunity," Jesse continued. "I thought it was going to be difficult trying to let her down easily. The guys, too. I doubt she'd accept no as a definitive answer. Now, I think I've come up with a way to get everyone on the same page without the risk of further questioning. That is, if you'll let me."

"How?" Alex asked breathily. She couldn't stop thinking about his lips, how they would feel against hers.

"Forty-three. Forty-two. Forty-one. Forty." Even the baseball boys had joined in on the counting on the other side of the bathroom door.

Jesse slowly raised his hand. He touched his fingers lightly to Alex's temple and traced a feather-soft line down over her cheekbone.

Every nerve ending in her body was like a live wire and every breath seemed to draw her closer to him.

"Twenty-eight. Twenty-seven. Twenty-six."

Jesse gently brushed her curls behind her ear and Alex felt the caress of his touch everywhere. He leaned closer, his lips hovering above hers. "May I kiss you?" It was nothing more than a whisper.

"Seventeen. Sixteen. Fifteen."

"Better hurry, Morganson," Bethany yelled over their countdown.

Alex barely heard her teammate over the sound of her own blood pumping through her ears. *May I kiss you?* She swallowed back her hesitation. That's all she had ached to do for weeks.

"Five. Four. Three."

"Yes." Alex licked her lips as the bathroom door flew open. But neither she nor Jesse noticed.

Jesse cupped Alex's cheek and closed the distance between them as Bethany growled an indistinguishable curse and the onlookers at the threshold hollered. Yet their comments didn't matter. Alex was lost to the feel of Jesse's soft lips on hers. The way he moved his mouth so gently, so affectionately. Captivating her. How he caressed her with his tongue, leaving her wanting more of him. She slid her arms around his neck, pulling him closer as his other hand wrapped around her waist.

Somewhere by the door, a firm voice broke though the chaos. "Come on, guys, I think they need a bit longer than seven minutes. Let's all give them some privacy."

Was that Tarzan Tim coming to their rescue?

"Fine then." Bethany's voice sounded so distant now. "He wasn't really that hot anyway."

The voices of their voyeurs became muffled as the bathroom door slammed shut and Alex lost herself again to Jesse's steamy kisses. While she relished the sensation of being cuddled in his strong arms, enjoying the tangy scent of him, the sweet taste of him, and the feel of his perfect abs beneath her fingers, Alex realised she'd been wrong about the sexy-costume memo. It might have been Halloween, a time for everyone to pretend to be something they're not, but in the end she hadn't needed an attention-grabbing costume to win over the guy she liked. Weirdly enough, she just had to be herself.

Be Sure to Check out all of Tammy Mannersly's Heart Stopping Romances

PERSUADING LUCY

You can't hide from destiny….

Callum Hawthorne is one of those lucky guys who seem to have it all. He's a wealthy property tycoon, the CEO of his family's company. He's handsome, intelligent and charming and has a gorgeous new woman on his arm every week. But there's one thing still missing – the love of his life, Lucy Spencer.

Fourteen long years ago, Lucy left for college and cut off all contact with Cal, leaving their mutual friend Madison as his only connection. That was until in his effort to save his deceased father's beloved Gold Coast property, The Calypso, Cal contacts Insight Marketing, the best advertising firm in Melbourne, and discovers his Lucy among the team.

Successful marketing executive, Lucy Spencer had managed to avoid her ex-best friend for nearly half their lives. Fearful of trusting him, loving him and having her heart broken all over again, Lucy tries to keep her distance from him, but discovers that there is a fine line between love and hate, and maybe – just maybe – Cal could be her inescapable destiny.

~Persuading Lucy is a SEMI-FINALIST for the prestigious Chatelaine Book Awards for Romance Fiction and will quickly become your new favourite read.

EXCERPT-

Cal was flabbergasted. What had happened? What had he missed?

Then, distracted by her outburst, he made another mistake and his grip on Lucy's wrist loosened slightly. As if sensing his lapse in control, she used the whole weight of her small frame to jerk herself free of his hold and with a triumphant sigh she began to back away.

"So, you orchestrated this together, did you? What, did you seduce Maddy too? Why can't you just leave me alone?"

Cal's gaze narrowed with concern. "What are you talking about, Luce?"

Worried that she'd run before he had a chance to explain, Cal reached out and took a step toward her. But, Lucy immediately backed farther away, taking two steps for his single stride.

"What did you give her to make her finally tell you where I was?"

Her fiery glare was enough to make his fingers ache to touch her, to soothe her. He hated seeing her in so much distress.

"Nothing." His voice was calm, pacifying. "She didn't tell me."

Lucy frowned and her gaze dropped from his, confusion clearly clouding her expression.

"But I—" She shook her head with irritation and glanced back up at him. "But how did you know that I'd be here?"

Cal smiled as he remembered the moment of pure serendipity, the second he'd seen her gorgeous face on the team's profile page on the Insight Marketing website. *Executive Manager Lucy S.*, it had read. Cal had tried searching the internet for her before, but to no avail. There had always been too many Lucy Spencers and he'd been convinced that she must have altered her name. Yet, this time he'd found her, so simply found her, as though the universe had finally pointed her out to him.

"Fate," he said confidently.

DRAWN TO HIM

The new doctor in town is attracting some attention, especially of the female persuasion, but art teacher, Erica Townsend is blissfully unaware until she ends up injured and in his office. Too bad she'd vowed to resist love—that traitorous emotion, the destroyer of lives—after numerous failed relationships. Something about Matt, about their electrifying connection has her wondering if he might just be...*the one*.

Dr. Matthew Garrick is tired of playing wing-man for his best friend. It isn't that he wishes to look for love, rather the opposite. But the eagerness of some of the single women in their small country town unnerves him. That is, until a certain stunning brunette appears in the waiting room of his medical practice. Her touch sparks something deep inside him, jolting his heart into a new rhythm and Matt makes it his mission to win's Erica love. Can he convince her to take a risk on him and what they share together?

As the good doctor strives to show Erica that love doesn't have to come at a price, his dangerous secret admirer threatens to prove otherwise.

Whoever said love wasn't dangerous?

EXCERPT-

Then it happened, that final breath, her lips snuck closer, brushing his, leaving a scalding spark, a blistering burn where they'd briefly, barely touched his skin—and then they were gone.

Matt wasn't exactly sure *when* he'd closed his eyes, but when he opened them again Erica had disappeared.

The *click* of the door handle had him turning around. She was halfway out of his office before she turned back to look at him, to give him that deadly sexy smile, making his insides smolder and ache with a want he'd never experienced before.

A torrent of thoughts whirled through his head, driven to swirl faster with the knowledge that in these final few seconds, his last words needed to leave an impression, a very good impression.

"Make sure to keep it clean."

Erica's gorgeous eyes glittered back at him, and then she was gone, heading back into the waiting room to see Melina and Jocelyn.

Make sure to keep it clean?

Matt could have died right then and there. He could have said anything, anything at all. He could have said he hoped she had a nice day. He could have mentioned he'd see her at the art class on Friday. Even the corniest *"That was nice"* would have been a better option. But, no, the doctor voice in his head had won out and his concern over wound care had been the final impression his suave self had been willing to make. No *"Thanks for the kiss, you beautiful babe,"* just

"Make sure you don't get dirt on your injured knee."

He slapped his hand over his face and closed his eyes.

A GARLAND AT BITTERBARK CREEK

He's found a new home with her family while his own holds secrets to her past…This heart-wrenching **300+** page rural romance novel will have you gasping and keep you guessing as mysteries unravel, and as Jack and Sophie discover whether their love for one another can survive the deepest of wounds and darkest of betrayals.

Had it not been for her cousin's wedding, Sophie Wendall would never have returned to Bitterbark Creek—her aunt and uncle's idyllic farm-stay on the outskirts of town. Twenty years ago, tragedy stole everything from her including her memory, leaving only secrets and lies. Now that she's back, there are just two things on her mind: to find out the truth of what really happened to her that day at the dam and to steer clear of the wicked Garland family and their charismatic son—the boy who broke her heart.

Jackson Garland is one of the few people who know what really happened to Sophie all those years ago, but he's terrified of sharing the truth. To do so would jeopardize his happy sanctuary and newfound home at Bitterbark Creek.

Upon reconnecting with Sophie, he realizes that while her extended family may have accepted him as one of their own, she's going to take a little more convincing. Although he tries to charm and distract her to keep his secrets safe, it isn't long before he's at risk of falling under her own tantalizing spell.

As children, their love for one another kept them close until a car accident took one life and hatred tried to steal another. But dark truths can't be hidden forever when ghosts from the past step into the light. Might the revelations be too daunting for them to handle? Or will Jack and Sophie finally put aside their family history and let love guide them into a future together?

A GARLAND AT BITTERBARK CREEK is about heartbreaking loss, rediscovering love and the healing ability of forgiveness and acceptance. If you love reading the novels of Mandy Magro, Alissa Callen, and Rachael Johns, then you will adore this heartfelt, second chance love story by award-winning author, Tammy Mannersly.

EXCERPT-

"I'm fine." Sophie winced. "But don't expect me to make conversation."

"Don't be antisocial." Laura hugged Sophie's narrow waist. "I know he'd love to catch up. He's always asking about you."

Sophie pushed out of her cousin's embrace. She knew Laura meant well, but Jack's opinion of her hadn't meant anything for a very long time. "Well, he can just keep on asking. I'm not walking down memory lane with that jerk anytime soon." She thrust a hand towards her mother. "Please just give me my bags."

Frowning, Angelica opened the trunk with a click of a button and handed her daughter a hefty duffle bag and a wheeled suitcase. As Sophie lifted the silver handle free from the luggage case and turned on her heel, she collided with a damp, rigid wall of masculine muscles. Recoiling in horror, she stumbled backwards until the heels of her boots hit the side of her suitcase. As she wobbled, a solid arm slid around her waist, keeping her upright.

"Whoa, there. I've had women fall for me before, but not usually this quickly."

The smooth male voice dragged Sophie's attention to a familiar gaze. Jack's cool blue eyes, like the winter sky at dawn, held her captive. The memory of a gentle, secret kiss beneath the shelter of a weeping willow played across her mind, until the beat of his pulse shook her to her senses.

"Hey there, Soph."

Embarrassed that she'd allowed herself to linger in his embrace, Sophie swiftly withdrew. His hand stayed on her hip, emanating an unsettling but strangely pleasurable tingling, so she smacked it away. "I can stand by myself, Jackson."

"Just trying to help, Soph." His stubborn square jaw tightened around the words.

AVAILABLE IN EBOOK AND PRINT WHERE BOOKS ARE SOLD.

ABOUT THE AUTHOR

Tammy Mannersly is an award-winning Australian author frequently praised for her heart-warming stories full of romance, dedicated friendships, and stunning Australian locations. All her books ensure a great Happily Ever After and a love story that will sweep you off your feet. Tammy has a Bachelor Degree in Creative Industries majoring in Creative Writing from Queensland University of Technology. She lives on the coast near Brisbane, Queensland and loves to write about her favorite Australian destinations.

You can find more information about Tammy and her

work on her website: www.tammymannersly.com or by visiting:

Facebook:
https://www.facebook.com/tammymannersly
Goodreads:
https://www.goodreads.com/author/show/16935790.Tammy_Mannersly
Instagram:
https://www.instagram.com/tammymannersly/
Twitter: https://twitter.com/TammyMannersly
Bookbub:
https://www.bookbub.com/authors/tammy-mannersly
Inkspell   Publishing:
http://www.inkspellpublishing.com/tammy-mannersly.html

Merger

By Jennifer Raines

DEDICATION

To experimentation, to exploring the new, and to the people in my life who've stretched my imagination

MERGER

"Hello, Matilda."

I jerk upright. Only one person says my name with *that* intimate growl.

Said.

Past tense. Six years past tense.

"How did you get in?"

Ludicrous to say, but shock upends you. You don't always know yourself and behave in unpredictable ways. I should know. My heartbeat shifts to staccato. Not a life sustaining beat.

Six years ago, I left Sydney three weeks before Christmas. Dropped everything when I got the call from the cops that my parents were dead. Didn't leave my younger brother Jon's hospital room except for bathroom breaks and to deal with the various officials who apparently own a piece of you after a tragic car accident. More than two hours sleep at a time eluded me.

"The concierge had my name."

"You're not Edwin Peters!" I sound semi-hysterical, but Ben Masters is the last person I expected.

I must be hallucinating. Six years ago, I was ready to go anywhere with Ben. Then I blocked him. Now, anxiety about the merger of the struggling *Treacy* stationery company with *PaperiaPlease* has triggered my deepest fantasy, that one day Ben will walk back into my life, and it'll be as if we've never been separated.

He looks the same. *No.* I force myself to study him. There are changes, more sophistication, a certain aloofness, a few threads of grey in his thick locks. Still, my heart takes flight.

"Why are you here?" *Here,* specifically, in Ian Treacy's office in a Sydney high-rise at the seedy end of the CBD on the day after Christmas?

"My family bought *PaperiaPlease.* I manage it."

He shrugs, and my stomach clutches from a physical memory so strong it hurts.

"When I heard that you're Ian Treacy's representative for the merger talks, I couldn't resist the temptation to see if it really is you."

Not like this. This isn't how I'm supposed to meet you again.

"I sometimes wondered if you were a figment of my imagination," he adds. "Shall we go?"

I turn, like some AI-generated version of myself, to collect my jacket. You sound the same, all husky drawl soaked in whiskey. You introduced me to fine whiskey. You beat me at chess. You swept me off my feet, gave me ten months of passion-infused love and laughter. I'm happy to see you.

And embarrassed. And terrified.

Silently, you usher me into the elevator, but the warm, woody scent you still wear speaks louder than words, of cuddles and comfort and wild desire. Jingle Bells on a slight delay echoing through the faulty Muzak system adds to my sense of discombobulation.

My brother was physically and mentally broken. For years, he worried if I was out of his sight for too long. Now we have a silent pact to work through the holiday period— our way of dealing with ghosts and demons.

Which are you?

Six years ago, I was too scared to trust Ben with my future. The stakes are as high now as then. I chose Jon then, because he was helpless. My boss' age and inability to innovate make him the vulnerable one now. A family friend, Ian, gave me this job, when everyone else showed me the door. Now he's trusting me to protect his legacy and the future of his employees. I can't let him down, no matter how much my heart aches with what ifs.

* * *

We dine at a small restaurant still festooned with Christmas decorations. A radiata pine tree threaded with fairy lights is tucked into a corner. Ian hopes to end this year on a high, giving me five days to get this deal done. Ben ushers me toward a booth. It provides privacy. *Intimacy?* His genuine smile for the waiter who takes our order evokes erotic memories which weaken my resolve.

Ben asks how I am. I deflect him with a question about his offer. He enquires about my family. I explain the company's present financial position in concise sentences that emphasize its strengths. I'm deliberately putting him at a distance. He's setting me up for chess annihilation—Fool's Mate. We met at the university chess club, and were never apart from day one.

"Ian's first condition is that all staff are retained." I sound ridiculous in the face of his monumental cool. He manages *PaperiaPlease*. He's calling the shots, and I'm playing catch-up.

"Does that include you? Will *you* work for me?"

Ben's urbane and unreadable, when there was a time I was attuned to his every expression. I'm blindsided by the sense of loss.

"Until tonight, I didn't know you'd be the new boss."

"Think about it now. If you keep your present position, you'll be working directly with me." His gaze holds mine, his voice dropping to a silky drawl. "You have a history of running when the pressure gets tough."

I *am not* going to cry. I'm not even going to react. I know nothing about you *now*. You might be married with ten children. Okay, ten children in six years is unlikely. But you must have a lover, lovers, a girlfriend, a wife. I suck it in. I made my decision all those years ago. Doesn't matter if I have regrets. Have always had regrets.

"Our past history has nothing to do with these negotiations. If, when everything else has been resolved, you don't want me to work for you, then that can be arranged. Let's end there tonight."

"And resume tomorrow?"

Resume means restart. *If only.*

"Ian Treacy should take over, now that you've replaced Mr. Peters." I force myself to make the offer, when even this small contact makes me hunger for more.

"Let's see if we can work together?"

Work? I was your friend, lover, and dreamed of being more. I want to tell you everything. I want your arms around me. I want your body heat, your tender lovemaking. But, as Ian's representative, I owe it to my boss to handle this professionally. I owe it to myself. I was a coward six years ago. This time, I can do something right.

"I'll meet you here at seven tomorrow night, Ben."

He studies me, his beautiful eyes assessing whether I'm telling the truth. "Okay."

I did that to him. Made him doubt me.

* * *

For three nights, I stick to business, loading spreadsheets and product brochures onto my laptop, taking him through the numbers, the areas where we've innovated in recent years.

"*Treacy's* have copied some of *PaperiaPlease's* strategies." He glances up from the screen. "Is that your influence?"

Yes.

Studying best practice and applying what I can, to thank my boss for giving me a chance. Ian needs this lifeline. His employees need this, And, damn Ben to hell—*PaperiaPlease* is best practice.

"*Treacy's* is a solid business with good potential."

"Then why the merger?"

"You know why. Ian needs capital to take advantage of new technologies without compromising the brand. And you're here because you're seriously considering investing."

Ben hasn't asked a personal question, hasn't offered me a lift home, hasn't touched me, even accidentally, since that first night. I want to scream, to grab hold of him, to beg for another chance.

"I'll get a proposal to Ian tomorrow, the thirtieth of December."

"Does it include all staff?" I hold my breath.

"Yes." Ben leans back in his chair, drumming his fingers on the table. "I've missed you, Matilda. Have dinner with me on Saturday night to celebrate?"

'*Missed me*'. I flop back in my chair, my heart flipping over. Then I remember. "I can't. That's New Year's Eve."

"Can't or won't?"

"My brother has a band. His singer's sick. I've promised to fill in. They can't afford to cancel without risking future gigs."

"I know what happened." His voice roughens, raising a past I've fought to push to the back of my mind during our business negotiations.

"Pardon." My head's still stalled on '*missed me*'. Words I've heard only in my dreams.

"I went to your house repeatedly. Then I saw the For Sale sign. I spoke to the neighbours. Your parents died, your brother was touch and go for months, you weren't even in Sydney. Your socials went blank."

"When you asked about my parents that first night, you already knew?" I'm struggling to catch up. I touch my tongue to dry lips, and his gaze settles on my mouth. He *missed me.*

"Why didn't you ask *me* for help?" Bewilderment clouds his voice, and guilt pushes hope aside.

"I wasn't Matilda Richards, carefree university student any more. I was Jon's legal guardian. I could barely think straight. I decided it was right to cut you out of my life."

I have his full attention now.

Shit, shit, shit. Time to tell him what I should have told him then. *I owe him the truth.*

I whisper the words. "I doubted that you'd still want me, love me, accept *us*."

He stills, shock creasing his features, then pain.

It's too late to take back what I've said, what I've done. The words I should say are stuck in my throat.

I was scared to trust your love. Your family's wealthy, I was destitute. I didn't want to become a burden.

Too late to discover it wasn't my decision to make. I should have given him the choice to be part of Jon's and my life. My insecurities sabotaged whatever might have been.

For a moment he just looks at me, emotions chasing each other across his face as he relives the past. He stands, closing the shutters on his thoughts with me on the outside. "I'll go."

Still, I catch his sleeve. To hold him in place? To make excuses? "What about the merger?"

Did I just ask that stupid question?

Right now, I don't care about the merger. I care that I locked Ben out.

"I'll submit my offer tomorrow, as promised." He shakes his arm free, his tone flat.

We'd both made promises. I walked away from mine without a warning or an apology. "I'm sorry, Ben."

I still love him. I questioned his love. I was sure of mine.

Tears run down my cheeks. Ben won't sabotage the merger. He's not a coward, *like me*. I was too shell-shocked to see it six years ago. I didn't see anything clearly six years ago.

* * *

On Saturday night, I don the uniform. Figure hugging black silk minidress. Check. Stilettos. Check. Purple smudges under my eyes from crying. Check. I can only hope the audience doesn't look too closely. Ben hasn't called me, won't call me. I hurt him and bumbled my explanation. At least, Ian was happy with the contracts, heaping praise on me, praise I don't deserve. Seeing Ben brought it all back, the pain…the love?

I don't want to sing tonight.

I can't let Jon down.

Can't let Jon down, can't let Ian down. The only person I've consistently let down is Ben. And myself.

Halfway through the night, I nod to the band and abandon the playlist.

"This next song is for an old friend."

I start a hauntingly beautiful love song. For Ben, but he'll never know. I stare out across the stage lights.

Is that Ben, or am I fantasizing again? He waves before moving to a table at one side of the room.

I'm deliriously happy for no reason. Except Ben's *here*. At the end of the number, I take a break. Applause rings around me, but I don't care. I step from the stage and walk to Ben's table.

"Great show."

"Thanks." I smile. Uncertain. "Ian's delighted with your offer."

He shrugs. "It's a good deal for us. Will you work for me?"

"Do you want me to?"

"Still don't trust me, Matilda?"

"It wasn't about trusting you."

"You didn't love me."

I move closer, so only Ben can hear me. "I loved you, but I didn't want to see your love die. I wasn't functioning normally. My fear tripped me up. It was my mistake, not yours."

"No, perhaps you were right. I did love you, but I imagined a carefree, romantic love. I might have hesitated about accepting all that responsibility." He stops my protest. "That's why I was so stunned when you told me. I needed time to think about that."

He'd loved me! *He's using past tense.* I killed his love!

"Tilly, it's time for the next bracket."

I gesture frantically to my brother. "Give me a minute."

"It's all right, Matilda. I'll be here until the end."

"I must finish the show." I plead for understanding.

"I've waited for you this long." He grins. His special grin, with that particular tilt to his mouth, that light in his eyes, reserved just for me. My heart beats double time. "I can wait a bit longer, that is, if you answer a question."

"The answer's yes."

I love you.

He leans forward to brush his lips across mine. "I haven't asked the question yet."

"It's still yes."

The band plays the opening chords of the next number. I see the promise in Ben's eyes, and take a risk, cupping his jaw with one hand, and settling my lips over his.

He wraps me in his arms, deepening the kiss, ignoring the wolf whistles of the crowd.

Don't Miss Any of Jennifer Raines' Sensuous Romances...Available in Ebook and Print!

TAYLOR'S LAW

Tell me a secret and I'll tell you a lie.

Ella Anderson adores her niece. Despite struggling to make ends meet, accepting her dying sister's request she raise Tessa as her own is a no brainer. Until she receives a summons from a legal goliath on behalf of a wealthy stranger claiming paternity and, potentially, custody of her child.

Jake Taylor has been ripped off one too many times. Yet the letter from a woman claiming his cousin fathered her child feels real. His aunt and uncle are desperate for a grandchild. When the child's aunt shows up in his office in place of the child's mother, he smells fraud.

Secrets and lies bubble to the surface, threatening Ella and Jake's growing attraction. In a minefield of divided loyalties, can Ella trust Jake to make the right decision about custody of Tessa?

Jennifer's book is great for fans of contemporary romances where attraction blossoms into breath-stealing passion, where mutual respect leads lovers to also being friends, and where humour and tolerance enliven a deep and abiding love.

Jennifer likes to think her readers get occasional hints of the deep passion of a Nora Roberts or the unshakeable loyalty of a Grace Burrowes where love conquers loneliness, distrust and fear.

EXCERPT-

"Who are you?" he demanded.

The tension in his liquid chocolate voice rippled through her. This man couldn't be Tessa's father. The ferocity of her denial rattled her. Every cell refused to accept he'd been her sister's lover. And some remnant of reasoned thought nagged at her. He'd have eaten Chrissy alive.

"Eleanor Anderson." With an effort, she gathered her professional poise. "Chrissy's sister. Ella. You must be Drew." She reached out a hand.

"You know damn well I'm not Drew."

"If you aren't Drew, who are you?" Off-balanced by his instant attack, she tried to steady her jumpy nerves. Withdrawing her hand, she turned to the older man, who was staring at Tessa. "Mr. Taylor, your letter requested Chrissy meet you here about Drew Browning's paternity and ..." She stumbled to a halt over the word "custody," then shook her head as a bizarre idea formed. "You can't be Drew?"

"I'm his father, Peter." His presence confused her further but confirmed the identity of the pirate king.

She stretched out a hand for a second time. "Then you must be Mr. Taylor. Good morning."

"Where's Chrissy?" Taylor demanded.

Before she could answer, Tessa's soft voice ricocheted around the room. "Mama's in heaven."

PLANTING HOPE

Can digging and weeding, planting, and pruning equal love?

Nursing is Holly Cooper's vocation, and her sanctuary, until she witnesses a murderous attack during emergency surgery. Her childhood fear of never belonging resurfaces. Untethered, she's following music festivals down Australia's eastern seaboard, sometimes working as a nurse, sometimes as a volunteer.

Reclusive gardener Christopher (Kit) Silverton needs a nurse for his half-finished research project: the therapeutic power of gardening. In plain English, can digging and weeding, planting, pruning, hacking, or any one of those activities help kids to heal after domestic violence? A survivor himself, he knows what it's like to live with pain, guilt, and relationships that end in tears.

When Kit's partner, and on-site nurse, is injured, she suggests her granddaughter, Holly Cooper, as a replacement. Holly has the qualifications, but Kit will need convincing that a pink and green haired free spirit has anything to offer the project.

As the garden develops, passion blooms between Holly and Kit. When security on the site is breached, Kit confronts his worst nightmare. Defending the kids and

Holly proves his critics right—violence lives within him. Can Holly overcome her own doubts to prove he's wrong?

Jennifer Raines's books evoke the romance of Nora Roberts' books but set in the sweeping Australian countryside. PLANTING HOPE proves that love can overcome demons and let our true self shine through. Don't miss this story that blooms like a garden of hope.

~The toughest issues, the tenderest hearts. What a lovely tale! ~ *Grace Burrowes about Planting Hope*

EXCERPT-

"You know the dog."

Holly recognised the voice of her caller from earlier in the day. Her gaze travelled up long legs and paused at the work-roughened hand holding the large cat basket where Max peered regally through the mesh. Continuing up, she found a broad chest, covered in a navy sweater knitted in an intricate pattern Mona reserved for those she was fond of. Holly's stare landed on a craggy, square-jawed face scowling at her. His frosty grey gaze suggested his mood hadn't improved. *How come Mona didn't mention her ripped, mid-thirties friend?*

"Christopher Silverton." She scrambled to her feet and offered a hand. "I'm guessing you looked after Bella and Max, as well as Mona."

He refused her offer of a hand, instead doing his own slow survey. She failed whatever test he'd set her. "I've driven past the house a few times today," he said. "But you weren't here."

"Just got here," she replied. The guy needed a personality bypass, but he'd done his second good deed for the day.

"It's after nine."

"Is it?" It could be a hair past a freckle for all Holly cared. She held out her hand. "Max."

"I fed them." He handed her the carrier. "I'll take you to the hospital."

Her eyebrows rose at the masterful tone. "That's not necessary."

"The least you can do is go and see your grandmother. Or"—he leaned closer and his nostrils twitched—"maybe you need a bath first."

"Advice noted." She set the carrier on the floor, then closed the door in his face, deliberately locking it. She braced herself—body and mind—for a pushback, expecting his pent-up irritation to explode in loud knocking or shouted instructions. Nursing had taught her a lot of men didn't take no for an answer. Her heart skittered against her chest. A lot of people didn't take no for an answer.

MASQUERADE

Fool me once...

Money won't bring LIAM QUINN'S father back, but it'll save his mother's home. A high-paying law partnership is in his sights. To win it, he needs to successfully land a project. Problem is the project requires absolute confidentiality, and he's just discovered his estranged identical twin is appearing life size on a billboard across the city. The second catch is a return to environmental law. His earlier career imploded after his lover was revealed as a mining company spy.

Researcher and soon-to-be-published romance author KATE TURNER needs a disguise. Maybe more than one. Her famous playwright father despises 'trashy' novels. Her ex-boyfriend mocked her 'dirty little secret', then stalked her when she left him. Her identical twin coaxes her into appearing on a billboard to prove she can be notorious and anonymous at the same time. No one connects the billboard model to the dowdy researcher Kate has become, and no one knows about her author pseudonym and second disguise as Ms. Sexy Romance.

Kate and Liam's lives collide when she's hired as Liam's research assistant. Liam's boss laughs off the billboard. Having doubles is the perfect cover for confidential field work.

A masquerade, a road trip, a steamy attraction, the sudden appearance of Liam's old lover, and Ms. Sexy Romance's unexpected arrival in the wrong place at the wrong time, and Liam and Kate discover the steps they took to protect their hearts might break them.

Award winning author Jennifer Raines' stories combine a love of romance with contemporary conflicts. Her writing is both relevant and heart-warming. Each story is a journey across the world. Jennifer likes to think her readers get occasional hints of the deep passion of a Nora Roberts or the unshakeable loyalty of a Grace Burrowes where love conquers loneliness, distrust and fear.

--"A Jennifer Raines romance will make you sigh in the best possible way!"-- Best Selling Author, Grace Burrowes

EXCERPT-

"Kate Turner meet Liam Quinn." George made the final introduction. The man's name provided the absolute confirmation Kate didn't need. Inhaling deeply, she met his gaze.

"Hello, Ms. Turner." He held her hand longer than

necessary, the living embodiment of all her least favourite stereotypes. An austere, charcoal-suited, silk-tied, face-chiselled-from-marble legal eagle who regarded her with the irritation of someone who'd found a worm in his perfect apple. The man packed speculation and suspicion into a simple handshake. "Do I know you?"

Have you ID'd me? Memo to self: you will not—repeat not—hyperventilate. Kate concentrated on simple inhalation and exhalation. In two-three; out two-three. Nice and steady. "I don't think so."

"You look familiar."

"I have that kind of face." She'd let her guard down, allowed herself to believe the gods were finally on her side—that she could work, write and live again free of shadows.

"I don't think so." He was persistent. "Maybe I've seen a photo?

"Unlikely." In two-three; out two-three-four-five. There was a Genosearch billboard on the route from the airport to Sydney's central business district. The public story was that Kate's identical twin, Anna, was the model featured in glorious colour on the billboard. Instead, Kate was the real billboard model, having abandoned her Ms. Dowdy Researcher disguise for the length of the photo shoot. "Call me Kate."

Had Liam seen through the costume granting her anonymity from every other observer?

AVAILABLE IN EBOOK AND PRINT WHERE BOOKS ARE SOLD.

ABOUT THE AUTHOR

Hi, I'm Jennifer Raines and you can find out more about me at https://jenniferrainesauthor.com. I write sensuous contemporary romances where passion and respect deliver happily-ever-afters. I write in third person dual point of view, so *Merger* is an experiment for me in first person point of view. I'd love to know what you think of it.

Sunset

(A Wild Horse, Wild Heart Origin Short)

By Christina Rhoads

SUNSET

By early evening, the scorching heat had begun to break, and the sky over the rodeo grounds softened to a dusty blue. Long shadows stretched across the dirt, and a warm breeze drifted through the chutes and holding pens, thick with the scent of sweat, hay, and manure.

Elsie stood at the fence line, one boot hooked over the bottom rail, her arms crossed. She was supposed to be stretching, reviewing her pattern, and focusing on her time in the show pen. But her gaze kept drifting to the warm-up arena, where a tall bay gelding was loping in circles.

The horse moved like a storm—tightly coiled, every muscle primed to explode. His chestnut coat gleamed in the sun, darker across the legs and haunches, nearly black below knee and hock. His head, marked by a long roman nose, was not beautiful but there was still something compelling about the horse. The rider didn't correct the horse, much. He didn't push, either. He just stayed with the horse, every movement quiet, deliberate. As if the rider was listening to something no one else could hear. The horse liked him. It was obvious. They liked each other, *trusted* each other. They were creating something magnificent together, horse and rider, and she didn't want to miss a moment of it. This level of unity was something she didn't see often at the drive-up rodeos. Of course her own horse knew her every thought, and almost moved without the cueing of her aids, but to see someone else ride the same way, made her feel that she somehow knew the man before even learning his name.

"Next up, Corbin Darkhorse, riding Ghost Dancer," the announcer said, his voice static over the speaker.

Elsie narrowed her eyes, intrigued. She'd heard the name before, maybe on a draw list or in passing from a judge, but this was the first time she'd seen him ride. And it was tough to look away.

A small child ran up the bleacher steps, just as horse and rider entered the show pen, making the whole apparatus shake. The horse started to scoot, tucking his tail, his ears pinned and his back tense. The nice lope giving way to something that would make a less experienced rider panic. His strides were off-tempo, jerky, like he was trying to shake something loose. But Corbin didn't flinch. He didn't force or brace. He just let the horse move through it, waiting for the tension to settle. His hands were quiet. His seat, anchored.

That kind of patience didn't show up often in the lower-level reining shows, especially here in nowhere Wyoming, where the less experienced rodeo riders only tried their hand at a reining pattern.

She almost didn't hear Willow come up beside her.

"Figured I'd find you here," Willow said, brushing dust off her jeans. "Isn't he the one with the rehab horse?"

Elsie didn't answer right away. She was still staring at Corbin guide Ghost Dancer through the last turn. The gelding's gait had smoothed out, not polished, but consistent, he was asking the horse to shift his weight onto his haunches as he set him up for a spin. The animal listened, one ear fixed on his rider, the other still focused on the bleachers.

"He's not just rehabbing the horse," she murmured, suddenly proud of this man she didn't even know. "He's giving him space to figure it out."

Willow tilted her head, a twinkle in her eye. "Didn't realize you were scouting cowboys?"

"I'm not." Elsie stepped down from the rail. "I just respect the ride." Suddenly annoyed with her friend, and herself, she wanted to shake off the feeling of something catching at her insides.

Willow didn't press, but Elsie could feel her watching with that familiar, knowing smirk. Knowing she was up to practice soon, Elsie headed off to the barn, miffed that Willow had broken the magic of watching Corbin and Sky Dancer's ride.

An hour later, Elsie was back at the trailer, unsaddling Sky. Her gelding was still hot from their run; his coat streaked with sweat. He was a sharp one—quick to react, but quicker to recover. Just like Elsie. Not bred for flash, but definitely gritty, and together they'd grown into a team.

Elsie rubbed him down carefully, working the sweat marks out with long, practiced strokes, then applying liniment and working her fingers across the delicate tendons. She didn't have help, not from family anyway. They'd never understood her love for horses-- too dirty, too expensive, too far outside their suburban world of soccer games and nursing school dreams.

So she did it alone. Booked her own entries. Taught herself patterns off YouTube when no one would coach her. Bought Sky as a yearling with money from mucking stalls after school. Every run, every win, was hers alone.

She didn't expect anyone to understand. She just needed them to stay out of her way.

"Nice ride. "The voice came from behind her, low, steady.

She turned and found Corbin standing just a few feet back, one hand resting on his belt, the other holding a long piece of hay. Out of the saddle, he looked even more sure of himself. His smile was dazzling when she met his gaze, and for a stunned second she couldn't think.

"Thanks," she said. "Sky's a handful, but he's fast and we're getting more confident in our stops."

He nodded toward the gelding. "He moves like he's got something to prove."

Elsie smiled faintly. "He does. Or *we* do."

Corbin stepped closer, carefully, letting his other hand drop to his side. "You train him yourself?" He was wearing a clean but worn shirt, the collar frayed and one of the pear snaps missing.

"Every step." She didn't mean it as a challenge, but it came out like one. The man was sidling up to her like she was a spooky colt. She wanted to know more about him, but his sudden proximity made her edgy. In fact, she wanted to ask him question after question about how he trained horses, who he looked up to, and maybe even what his dreams were, but her natural reserve made her wait. It was always better to be careful with cowboys.

Corbin just nodded again, thoughtful. "I could tell. You two move like you've been arguing for years."

Elsie laughed, caught off guard. "That's accurate."

He held out a hand. "I'm Corbin Darkhorse."

"Elsie," she said, shaking it. His grip was firm, his hand warm and rough with calluses. Not the kind from a gym—the kind from a lifetime of reins and ropes and barn gates. "But not really arguing so much as learning to 'communicate,' know what I mean?" That *was* a challenge and when he looked up, his eyes were laughing. He obviously enjoyed one.

"You from around here?" she asked, moving away from him and putting the horse between them. He was too close, too big, too much suddenly. She could smell horse on him, and saddle soap, and something wild and fresh like mountain spruce.

He shook his head. "Grew up in Montana. My mom's still out there. She raised me and my brother mostly on her own. We've been around horses since we could walk." He added the last as a sort of afterthought, and then flashed that megawatt smile her way again. He hadn't mentioned the reservation, as if he was daring her to ask. But she wouldn't. She'd been raised better than that and he looked like a man who would tell her what he wanted to tell anyway.

"You on the circuit as a reining rider?" She asked. Shifting the conversation back to safer topics.

"Trying to be. Just started doing more training work this past year. Mostly rehab, groundwork, re-starts. I pick up some ranch work when it's slow."

He said it all without pretense, like it was just the truth and nothing more, but then he looked up and she saw the fight in his eyes and something else, like he was taunting her to laugh at him, tell him he wasn't good enough. Elsie appreciated his dare .

"Ghost Dancer's not an easy ride," she said. "But you handled him well."

Corbin turned away from her and toward the arena, where the last of the riders were wrapping up. "He's not ready yet. Still scared of his own thoughts most days. But there's a good horse under all that."

She nodded. "I saw it."

A quiet pause passed between them. "His owners want him out this year," he admitted. Playing with a small rock with the toe of his boot. She could understand that too-- the push to pay bills, keep folks happy, produce results. What made it hard was that there was an animal, living and breathing, and certainly feeling, involved in the whole situation.

"You ride solo?" he asked. "Didn't see anyone helping you tack up or even coaching you in the warm-up."

Elsie's jaw tightened. She hated admitting how little her family cared. "I'm on my own." But the fact that he'd noticed her, watched her warm-up made her smile.

He didn't ask why. Didn't offer sympathy, either. Just nodded like it made perfect sense.

"That makes two of us," he said.

Sky nickered softly behind her, drawing Elsie's attention. She checked the gelding's chest, still hot under her flat palm, and damp.

"You heading to Cody next weekend?" she asked.

"My old stomping grounds. Yeah, that's the plan," Corbin said. "Not sure if Ghost Dancer's ready, but he needs the exposure. The noise. The crowd." He stretched his hands out and she noticed how long his fingers were. The nails were evenly cut and the tips of his fingers blunt and symmetrical, slightly pale on the insides.

Elsie teased. "Come for the chaos, stay for the experience."

He grinned. "Exactly." Relaxed, he seemed in no hurry to leave and she enjoyed it, just the two of them and the horse. Forget the rest of the people, looking questions at her as she talked to the tall cowboy. Hopefully Willow wasn't watching from her fancy trailer.

She picked up a lead rope and started unclipping Sky off the trailer. "I'm chasing the year-end points. It's not much, but… it means something to me." She didn't add that the prize money would keep her going through next year, even if she had to spend the winter in Denver teaching walk-trot lessons to middle aged women with too much lip filler.

Corbin didn't say anything right away. The loud speaker was going again, and the roar of the crowd told her some of the more popular events, like bull riding, were starting up under the glare of the lights.

Night settled in around them, and she hadn't even noticed. She reached in one-handed to grab the wool cooler from inside the horse trailer, and slung it over Sky's back. Corbin grabbed the other side and straightened it out over the horse's broad back. Sky bent his head around and sniffed the man's hands, slowly, then swung around to touch her hand. 'He's alright' the touch seemed to say.

"You ride like someone who doesn't wait for permission," he said, no leadup. His voice quiet as he was watching the arena and crowd.

She paused, blinked, then studied his face. "Is that a compliment?"

"It's an observation," he said. "But yeah. It is." She could see the smile even in the failing light.

That buzz in her chest, she wasn't sure if it was from adrenaline, or the way his words made her feel seen in a way no one else at these rodeos ever bothered to.

"Well," she said, brushing her hands off, "I'd better go walk a few laps with him, he's heating back up." So was her face, but she hoped he wouldn't notice as she ducked her chin and let her hat brim shield her. *Thank goodness for the coming darkness.*

Corbin stepped back. "I'll come walk him with you, Elsie."

She met his eyes—steady, warm, playful. He was goading her.

"That's okay, I'll be fine." Her answer was automatic.

"Sure, I know you will." He slid his hands in his pockets. "But maybe I *want* to come."

She felt the brush of a light breeze along her neck and with it a knowing shifted deep inside her. When he laughed, her short and cutting retort balled up in her throat. Elsie simply smiled and shook her head.

"Sure, you come find me tomorrow when you leave, and we'll caravan up north. It's good to have company on that stretch of highway. You can have your quiet moment with your horse."

She liked he knew she needed this time with Sky, to both settle after their ride. She also *could have* told him Willow and her parents had offered the same thing, but she didn't. She needed him to want to come with her. She was not the sort of woman that chased. No he would have to follow her, that's the only way this could work, she knew this about herself.

And as she led Sky toward the night and the last of a pink sunset long gone, she glanced back once, just for a second. Corbin had already turned away, heading toward his trailer. Not hurried. Not looking back.

Still, something had shifted. She could feel it—not like fireworks or lightning, but something deeper, like a tremor deep in the earth, and she feared. Now was the time to tell him no, to walk away on her own. This was a man who could break her heart.

Don't Miss the Rest of the Story in Wild Horse, Wild Heart

WILD HORSE, WILD HEART

"Elsie?" the dust settled, and she took a deep breath, gathering her anger around her. Carefully, trying not to let her limp show, she turned toward the now famous natural horsemanship trainer. The Lakota cowboy, Corbin Darkhorse, and the very first man she had ever loved, stood watching her. He was even more handsome than she remembered: dark hair, dark eyes, with long-fingered hands weathered by the sun and wind. She swallowed a mouthful of dirty words and wondered why he had to be here, on this day, as she picked up her mustang for the competition.

Forgiveness had never been one of Elsie Rosewood's strengths, and Corbin could see she hadn't changed over the last ten years. In fact, she looked as wild, angry and stubborn as the mustang pacing in the corral behind her. His mind filled abruptly with the old image of Elsie's face bloodied, as a previous wild horse threw her to the ground and trampled her limp body. Ten years was a long time to run, and Corbin knew if he ever wanted to have peace, and the trust of the only woman he'd ever loved, then he would have to prove how much he had changed.

The only thing standing in the way of a once- in-a-lifetime love is a Mustang Training Competition, $100,000, and a past neither forgotten nor forgiven.

EXCERPT-

The wild horse reared and then lunged toward Elsie. She stepped back just as the mustang crashed into the steel stock panels. A cloud of dust enveloped her and the horse; for several long moments, they were alone in a world of golden haze.

The mustang stood perfectly still, breathing hard. She could see fear and anger in his eyes; she felt her own heart beating with similar anguish. Very slowly, she reached out her hand, hoping the horse would sniff her damp fingers.

"You always draw the crazy ones," she heard from behind her. The golden moment disappeared as the dust settled and the noise of the stockyard rushed to flood her ears. The mustang spun away from Elsie and she pulled her hand back.

She didn't want to turn and see the man standing behind her. At the sound of his voice, she was again seventeen, and falling in love for the first time.

A trickle of sweat made its way down her back and she forced her fisted hands to open at her sides.

Finally, she did turn, but only after straightening her shoulders and smoothing her face of any emotion. Corbin Darkhorse stood taller and broader than she remembered. There was a smug smile on his expressive lips. "You look good, Elsie," Corbin said. "You're training horses again?" He stared at her with his dark eyes and that slow, suggestive smile she remembered all too well. For a long moment, Elsie looked into his eyes, then her mind switched on and she jerked away, swallowing a mouthful of dirty words.

UNDER THE MOUNTAIN STARS

After the death of her mother and end to her troubled marriage, Lenora Ranvier is feeling more alone than ever before. She takes her aunt and uncle up on their offer to come and live on their failing cattle ranch in the Montana Mountains.

Lenora hopes to grieve and start over but has no plans to fall in love again. All that changes the moment she meets Clay Darkhorse, Lakota cowboy and foreman of Bear Dance Ranch.

Clay knows Lenora is the woman for him as soon as he sees her climb out of her pickup truck, exhausted and beautiful. He slowly wins over Lenora by taking her on long night horseback rides into the starry mountains but both Lenora and Clay have past traumas to heal before they can freely love again.

Joining forces they convert the ranch from a struggling cattle operation into a swanky guest resort. But Lenora and Clay must learn to trust each other if they are to share a love as true and strong as the mountains in which they live.

EXCERPT-

Despite the slow pulse of a headache, Lenora did not want to leave Clay. What she really wanted was to sit with him quietly, to show him she loved him more than she feared a broken heart. She needed a quiet night to say those words to him; a night to ride in the mountains, to feel the brush of stars and the smell of pine sap on the breeze. Instead, she went to his bedside, and with the nurse, his mother, her aunt, uncle and his brother all watching she bent and kissed his pale lips. When she pulled back his eyes were open, and that half smile she so loved slowly appeared on his face.

"Maybe I should tell those young colts to try and kill me more often." Clay said. "Seems you like me better hobbled and in bed."

Was it her imagination, she wondered, or was he flirting with her in front of his mother. Her face was hot, and she could not look up from the bedsheet.

"Please, don't ever let it happen again," Lenora said.

AVAILABLE IN EBOOK AND PRINT WHERE BOOKS ARE SOLD.

ABOUT THE AUTHOR

Christina Rhoads is a romance novelist and horse lover who makes her home in Indiana with her husband, dog, and three fat horses. When she isn't crafting love stories on the page, she's hosting weddings at her inn, where real-life romance fills the air.

Dear Readers,

Everyone at Inkspell is grateful for you, the reader, during this holiday season. We are romantics at heart and enjoy sharing our stories with you. Inkspell's Enchanted Holidays is a chance to delve deeper into a few of our favorite stories and revisit some amazing characters but it's also a chance to meet some new to you authors who just might have a wonderful story for you to fall in love with.

So, please enjoy this labor of love and visit our website or socials to find your next favorite author or book.

Be Enchanted,

Inkspell Publishing

ABOUT INKSPELL PUBLISHING

Inkspell Publishing began as a dream in 2012 after a number of other publishing houses closed. Slowly, through the years, Inkspell has grown yet still retains a family feeling, as we help authors reach their dreams!

Inkspell has over 100 current releases and many upcoming releases in a variety of genres from Young Adult to Contemporary, from Paranormal Romance to Science Fiction Romance, Holiday stories and weddings. Inkspell Publishing even has free reads, some of which tie into our series books.

You see there's something for everyone. Our goal is to produce quality books that appeal to a wide variety of readers. We are always looking for quality stories and driven authors. You can reach us at http://www.inkspellpublishing.com.